MISSION CRITICAL

A Cold War Novel

BY

Jamie Fredric

Mission Critical

This is a work of fiction. Names, characters, places, and incidents are the product of the author's imagination or are used fictionally. Any resemblance to actual events, locales, or persons, living or dead, is entirely coincidental.

Definition:

BUDWEISER -

1. An alcoholic drink

2. Insignia - Anchor/Trident/Eagle/Pistol
an anchor represents the Navy, a 'Trident' the sea, an eagle 'Air' and a pistol--always cocked, always ready--represents land.

Sea...Air...Land----the three operating environments of the U.S. Navy SEALs.

Prologue

The Sea of Japan -

Nervously, he drummed his fingers against the wall. His contact aboard the *Rachinski* was late and he worried. It wasn't like the KGB. Impatience aside, Russia's mole was in his glory, finally in his element. He was about to use all the skills he'd been taught, and suddenly, he wanted to scream out his Russian name, but instead, he spoke quietly. "Alexei Pratopapov! That's who I am." He would love to be there, wishing he could see the faces of the Americans when it was all over. But if all went as planned--and he had every confidence that would be the case--he would not have the pleasure to see their faces nor the opportunity to tell them, "Yes, it was me. I did this to you."

He stretched his arms overhead, feeling secure in his hiding place. He sniffed the air, imagining he smelled coffee. A good, strong cup of coffee would hit the spot, his one American vice, he admitted. He would miss it once he was back in his homeland. He had lived among the Americans for so many years, but his love for Mother Russia never wavered. Schooled in English from the age of three, he was still a young boy when he left his beloved Odessa, already being groomed for the day his country would need his services. *Odessa--the "Pearl by the Sea,"* he smiled, longingly. After all these years, would he even recognize it? Would he be able to adjust to Russian life again? Life in Russia was very different than in America, he admitted, especially after all the years gone by. But his superiors had promised him so much upon his return. He would not have to worry about money or security.

Unfortunately, he would have no one to share it with, at least not with his American wife. He pictured an official Navy car pulling into the driveway, a chaplain and Navy officer ringing the doorbell to his house on Sycamore Drive. There would be a brief memorial service and Katherine would be given a folded American flag. The United States Government would compensate her every month. After all, that's why he contributed to the Survivor's Benefit Fund, was it not?

A brief moment of despondency reached into his heart, but immediately he jolted himself back to reality, his thoughts angering him. Russians in his position did not feel sorry for themselves or others. It was time for him to begin thinking and feeling like the Russian he was. He jumped, startled by the crackling noise. He spoke into the walkie-talkie. "Yes, I'm here." No codes were being used, so the conversation was kept to a minimum.

"Our Chinese comrades have verified their position. They have agreed to our terms and conditions. We are going forward," the gruff voice aboard the *Rachinski* stated.

Alexei's heart pounded; his breathing was heavy. "I'm prepared."

"I will contact you tomorrow at our designated time. We will discuss the details. Comrade Gregorov has asked me to pass on his wishes for a successful mission."

Alexei envisioned the KGB bureau chief, and answered, "I understand. Convey my respects to our colonel and thank him."

He pressed the button on the walkie-talkie, then rewrapped it in the towel. He slid it back inside the small fan vent and retightened the screws on the louvered cover. Opening the door slowly, he looked up and down the passageway while staying hidden inside the closet. The Damage Control locker was a fairly safe place to hide, since it was only used by the fire fighting team to store their suits, hoses, OBA's (oxygen breathing apparatus), and devil's claws, used to tear apart mattresses that were on fire. Checking one more time to make sure no one was around, he locked the door, then began strolling down the passageway, arms locked behind his back.

He'd become a familiar site, roaming different areas of the ship, his "insomnia" once again preventing rest. "Poor bastard," they'd say noticing his bloodshot eyes in the morning. He would hear their comment and smile inwardly. One or two eyedrops of saltwater...and the charade would continue.

Chapter One

Washington, D.C.
Saturday, January 25, 1975

Powerful arm strokes and flutter kicks propelled the swimmer forward effortlessly, the water streaming over his shoulders, creating a mass of white turbulence in the pool's outside racing lane. Having grown up in the small town of Jenner, California, in Sonoma County, water became another way for him to release his pent up energy, whether it was hitting the surf along the coast or racing his friends in the Russian River. Today, he raced against no one but himself.

A voice echoed in the domed aquatic center. "Commander! Commander Stevens!"

The swimmer stopped and began treading water. As he shook water droplets from his head, he spotted the ensign standing at the edge of the pool's blue tile.

"Commander, I've got an urgent message for you. You're to report to Admiral Morelli on the double. He's waiting for you in his office, sir." Ensign Jason Pritchard was a bit short of breath after his run across the parking lot; the smell of chlorine seemed stronger as it hit his senses. He wrinkled his nose as he brushed the snow from his shoulders, then blew warm breath into his hands. The Admiral's young aide resembled a child playing grownup, with a black raincoat that nearly dwarfed him. The epaulettes on his raincoat and cap brim were spotted with snowflakes.

Water dripped from Commander Grant Stevens' 6'1" frame as he climbed the ladder at the deep end of the pool. He had a swimmer's build, narrow waist and hips, emphasizing his muscular shoulders. He reached for a folded towel on the wooden bench.

"Do you think I'll have time to change, Mr. Pritchard?" he asked, smiling.

"Uh, yes, sir. Of course, sir. I'll just phone the Admiral to tell him I found you."

"Very well."

The ensign started to leave, then hesitated, deciding he'd better get more specific information, knowing the Admiral the way he did.

"Excuse me, sir, but what time shall I tell him you'll be there?"

Grant gave his black submariner watch a quick glance, calculating he could make it in thirty minutes. "Tell him I'll be there by 1830, Ensign."

"Yes, sir."

"By the way, Jason, how did you know where to find me?" he asked with a raised eyebrow.

"It was the Admiral, sir. He suggested that I look here first. May I go now, sir?"

"Go ahead, Jason."

Ensign Pritchard saluted, and then quickened his pace as he headed for the hallway in search of a pay phone, his once shiny black shoes splashing in the puddles along the pool deck. He made a mental note to clean his shoes before the Admiral saw him.

Grant rubbed the towel over his wet, dark brown hair and watched the young officer splashing smartly along the deck, off to complete his task for Vice Admiral Eugene Morelli. He had to appreciate the ensign's sense of urgency, already aware of the fact that he'd better not piss off the Vice Admiral. Grant had experienced it one time himself, early on during his own stumbling, bumbling days as a "butter bar" ensign, referencing the thin, single gold bar worn on a shoulder board.

He threw the soaked, white towel over his shoulder and laughed to himself as he went to the showers. Ensign Pritchard didn't realize it now, but one day he'd eventually learn that 'Ball-Buster' Morelli was really a pretty good guy.

He stepped under the shower's spray and closed his eyes, his mind traveling back in time, when he and Morelli first met. Grant was right out of Annapolis, assigned to the Operations Department on his first ship, the guided missile cruiser Seattle. Morelli, then a commander, had been aboard for ten months. Grant's tour aboard the cruiser was cut short when he received his new orders to report for UDT (Underwater Demolition Team) Basic training in Coronado. Although their meeting had been brief, it was an impressionable one for the young officer. For a senior and junior officer to develop a close friendship was unusual, to say the least, but Morelli had quickly recognized Grant's talents and enthusiasm. And their friendship was due in part because of Morelli's own son, who was a Navy helo pilot and the same age as Grant. James Vincent Morelli, 30 years old, was stationed in Ben Cat, located in the stinking Rung Sat Special Zone, a major helo base for operations. A VC attack on the base camp ended his life nearly six years ago. Grant seemed to fill some of the void left in Gene Morelli's life.

He threw open the door and ran into the cold night air. "Better get your ass in gear, Stevens!"

A deep rumbling sound from the 454 'Big Block' engine of his 1974, black, Corvette Sport Coupe bore into the evening stillness as Grant pulled out of the parking lot. Within fifteen minutes he was at his destination, turning into the parking slot marked by a painted metal sign, "Special Operations Officer."

Wide, steel-belted Goodyear tires skidded on a patch of ice hidden by the fresh snow swirling around the blacktop. The Vette came to a stop at a slight angle within the painted white lines. Yellow letters, 'JSTDOIT', stood out clearly beneath the light of the California license plate. He got out, locked the door, and adjusted his cap as he leaned into a biting wind. How he missed the warm days on Silver Strand in San Diego, the infamous beach where SEALs did a portion of their training. On the other side of the coin, whether the seas were rough or calm, those miserable night swims in the waters of the Pacific were now just a memory.

"Christ! It's cold! Damn this weather!" Then he had to laugh, "You're turning into a wimp, Stevens!" Out of self-defense, he immediately broke into a fast jog, his bridge coat flapping open as he headed in the direction of the office building and his appointment.

Located off the Baltimore-Washington Parkway in Anne Arundel County, not far from the National Security Agency (NSA), the four-story structure was completely non-descript. A dismal gray color, the concrete and stucco building was featureless and plain, but unseen to outsiders, subterranean offices existed, containing an elaborate communications' intelligence network. Within the structure's walls were the Offices of the Naval Investigative Service.

The elevator lurched as it came to a stop at the fourth floor, the doors hissing as they parted. Grant rushed off, glancing at his watch, and giving himself a reprimand for cutting his timing so damn close. At the far end of the hallway he could see the light shining through the frosted glass of the office door. The closer he got, he started hearing the 'clicking' of the yeoman's typewriter keys as they struck the paper curled against the platen. As many times as he'd been here, he still wondered how anyone could sit in an office, typically decorated in the usual Navy style with pea-green bulkheads. He couldn't imagine how Second Class Yeoman Alex Gardner managed to look at puke-colored bulkheads all day long for the past fifteen months of his assignment.

Gardner looked up from his IBM Selectric typewriter, the stub of a sharpened No. 2 pencil tucked behind his ear. Recognizing Grant immediately, he gestured and said, "Go right in, Commander. The Admiral's been expecting you."

"Thanks, Alex." The tone in the petty officer's voice made him worry that this wasn't about to be an amusing evening. He immediately detected the distinct odor of a cigar seeping from under the Admiral's door. It was hard to believe Morelli still had those damn Havanas.

Before Grant left on his last job in Cuba to do a photo check of the island's ports, Morelli made one of the few personal requests he'd ever asked of Grant. He wanted a box of Cohiba cigars. The superior quality cigar, extremely difficult to obtain, was expressly used by a privileged few, Castro always having a supply, serving them to heads of state and diplomats. Morelli had two reasons for making the request: first, the cigars were his favorite, and second, it was a test to see if the Navy SEAL could actually do it.

Confident, Grant had answered, "Piece of cake, sir." Then he asked with a crafty smile, "By the way, which size? Grande?"

Now, standing in front of the office door, Grant removed his cap, tucked it under his left arm, and then knocked, hearing the Admiral's voice, "Come!"

"Evening, Admi--"

"Grant! Want you to meet Sam Phillips, one of

the 'Cowboys in Action.'"

CIA Agent Phillips gave the Admiral a disapproving sideways glance as he stood and reached for Grant's hand. "Commander." Grant just nodded.

Admiral Eugene Morelli, Chief of Naval Investigative Service, shoved the thick manila folder to the corner of his desk toward Grant. "Here, take a look at this. The Agency has some scoop that this is beginning to take on the look of a fast 'dance card.'" Morelli referred to the name given to after action reports.

Grant looked at the folder stamped with half inch red letters 'TOP SECRET', and then did a quick assessment of the CIA agent, glancing back at Morelli who picked up on Grant's expression and chuckled to himself. The ache in his right shoulder made him remember the time Grant pulled him out of a burning chopper during a training exercise in Virginia that went haywire. Obviously, that was his personal reason for liking Grant. On a professional level, he knew Grant was the best covert 'frog' in the Teams or any of the so-called agencies. With his extensive experience as intelligence officer, coupled with his being a Navy SEAL with more than 60 combat patrols and 13 years covert ops background, Commander Stevens was one of the premier operators the country had at its disposal.

Grant hung his cap on the wooden coat rack by the door, then went to the desk and reached for the manila folder. He eyed Phillips again, noticing what he thought was a bad suit, and the overcoat seemed a bit much.

His brow furrowed as he scanned the first few pages of the printed report, then he started pacing back and forth across the carpeted office. He dropped the folder on the edge of the desk. "Admiral, can we talk privately?"

Phillips stood abruptly and excused himself, commenting out of the corner of his mouth, "Hey, when you rope chokers get your act together, buzz me back in when you're ready. I'll be in the outer office." The door slammed.

Grant spun around and blurted out, "Admiral, what's that clown doing here?"

Morelli had a knack at pushing the right buttons. "Look, I know you're still miffed about Cuba, and the Lumumba fiasco didn't help your opinion of the Agency either."

"Damn right, Admiral. You know it's the covert operators and the special ops guys that come under fire and take the heat because they're fed old intel, sometimes three weeks old. And that's not good enough, sir."

Morelli noticed the fire in Grant's eyes. If anything got Grant Stevens' ire it was incompetence, especially if it meant losing men or caused a mission's failure.

"I agree, I agree," nodded the Admiral, "but I think you need to hear this one. Will you do that for me?"

Grant yanked the folder off the desk. "Yes, sir...I'll listen." He sat in the big, leather chair, purposely selecting it over the uncomfortable wooden straight-back. His anger subsided as he became thoroughly engrossed in the report.

Normally a speed reader, Grant let his mind take in every word, never stopping, skipping nothing. "Jesus Christ!" He shot a quick glance at Morelli. "Uh, sorry, sir."

Morelli tugged on the skin sagging around his jawline, something that was becoming a perpetual habit. "No need. That's my sentiment exactly. Now, let's talk."

"Uh, why don't you buzz Phillips back in, sir? I promise I'll be good." He flashed Morelli a shit-eatin' grin through perfect, white teeth.

Morelli pushed the buzzer on the intercom and shook his head. Phillips came back in and sat in the wooden chair. Grant was across from the ornate walnut desk, the folder still gripped in his hand, concern in his eyes. "From the report, I see the situation's gotten worse over the last 72 hours. Any ideas, sir?"

The gray-haired senior officer reached for the cut crystal lighter on the corner of the desk blotter. Gnawing on the cigar tip, he looked at the younger officer then at the CIA agent. He relit the Lanceros panatela, then leaned back in his swivel chair, blowing a steady stream of white smoke across the desk, pointing the cigar at Grant.

"Agent Phillips has some information indicating the Russians and Chinese have expressed considerable interest in our latest weapons' platform."

Ignoring Phillips, Grant replied, "As long as the

CIA has known one was in bed with the other, why do they need us? They have operators--"

"That's why I called you in, Grant!" the cigar-smoking officer cut in sharply. Morelli leaned forward and rested his arms on the desk, the cuffs of his white shirt rolled back, revealing smeared black residue along the edges. He stared hard at the 36 year-old Navy officer. "Look, you're the best intel officer here at NIS, and water-borne ops isn't the Agency's best hand. We need a plan, and we need it pronto!"

Grant ran the back of his hand along his chin, realizing he needed a shave, and positive Morelli noticed. "Guess I'll ask the obvious question, sir. Is the *Bronson* part of the task force?"

Morelli nodded. "She is now. She joined up with them two days ago."

Grant turned and looked at Phillips. "When did you get the China news?"

"About three weeks ago. We only got confirmation from the Russkie side yesterday."

Grant glanced at the folder then up at Morelli. "Any place special you want me to start, Admiral?"

"SecDef and the Joint Chiefs are meeting tomorrow at 1030 hours. I'd like you to have something ready to present to them. Can you be there, too?" he asked Phillips.

"I can be," Phillips answered. He unwrapped a stick of Wrigley's Spearmint gum, folded it into thirds, and then popped it into his mouth.

"Good. It's settled then," Morelli stated.

Grant's thoughts were traveling at warp speed,

the intensity in his brown eyes making it obvious to the Admiral that a scheme was already in the works.

Morelli flicked the ash from the stub of the cigar into an ivory ashtray. He walked to the window, staring across the nearly deserted parking lot, paying little attention to the snow accumulating on the fourth story window ledge. He absent-mindedly drew a zigzag pattern with his finger across the moisture forming on the glass, and with urgency-laced words he said, "I've got all night, Commander."

Grant immediately recognized his old friend's deep concern just from the sound of the word "Commander."

Morelli turned, took a deep breath, and then stared directly at Grant. "Now, I know you've already got something on your mind. Let's hear it."

CHAPTER TWO

Off The Northeast Coast of Japan

Cruising at zero four five degrees, 2,500 yards off the carrier's starboard bow, the USS *Bronson*, DDGR-1, was making her first deployment under extraordinary circumstances. She never got a customary shakedown cruise after her maiden voyage...she was needed now. Her 4,000 tons and 325 foot length sliced through the water with a pronounced bow measuring 49 feet above the surface of the water. Her mean draft, 22 feet under the waterline, was impressive. Most ships delve deeper--she was built for speed. She had a cruising speed of 24 knots and a top speed that no one talked about, unless they belonged to the proper group. It was said, though, that she could do in excess of 45 knots. Out of 102 commissioned destroyers in service during 1975, she was the smallest and sleekest, but the most advanced destroyer in the world. The *Bronson* possessed capabilities beyond the imagination. This one ship had the ability to deal with and defeat any nation's arsenal of weapons, whether airborne, landlocked, or underwater, conventional or nuclear. Then, to add insult to injury, she could launch either a conventional or nuclear response within seconds of detecting a threat. All the missiles she carried onboard were undetectable. She was rigged to confuse, avoid, deter, destroy, and survive. Once her power was officially published, her very existence would forever instill the fear of God into any aggressor. Everyone realized this cruise might be when she would have no choice but to let her power be known.

What also made this a remarkable display of modern technology was that the USS *Bronson* had no crew, except for one. Her "crew members" were thousands of miles away, in Kodiak, Alaska. The secure network that allowed the *Bronson* and Kodiak to communicate was a scrambled, modern system that changed codes every hour. At an exact, predetermined time, encoded cards, the size of credit cards, were inserted into a panel, one on the *Bronson*, the other at Kodiak. No one, no modern equipment could decode or intercept the signals. This security for the *Bronson* was extraordinary because she possessed a weapon that was described only as the ultimate enforcer, far too advanced for its time, the most lethal weapon the world had ever known.

The concept had been around for more than three decades, the initial idea conceived by Dr. Forrest Wentfield, one of the physicists who had been recruited for the Manhattan Project and the development of the atomic bomb. Although a brilliant individual, his love of science fiction bordered on fanatical. It was from the stories of the futuristic heroes, Buck Rogers and Flash Gordon, that Wentfield developed his ideas while teaching physics at Georgetown University. He learned how the basics for capturing and using nuclear energy should be designed. From this the Satellite Neutron and Gamma System (SNAGS) was born, and the driving force for the development of the *Bronson*.

The ship carried no special launch technology topside that would arouse curiosity. Kept below deck was a simple reflecting communication's dish. Located just forward of the bridge, the launcher rails, once used for the supersonic surface-to-air TARTAR missile, were now used to raise and point the SNAGS. As SNAGS rose up on the rails, the onboard operator had the capability to aim it no more than a distance of eight miles. For longer ranges, the Alaska unit controlled the energy burst and satellite tracking vectors, sending the coordinates to the *Bronson*. The operator onboard simply had to pull the trigger once the dish was pointed at the satellite.

The SNAGS could radiate gamma and neutron rays captured from a nuclear reactor system in a separate array of filters that could reflect and traverse the particles and rays of radiation into a narrow beam. These would be funneled through an advanced accelerator that allowed the small satellite dish to pulse a solid beam of energy loaded with neutron and gamma rays. This refined beam would be sent through the dish. Its use could be 'line of sight' or bounced off a satellite deep in space. Its gamma and neutron energy would be reflected from the satellite to a surface target and the combined radiation would penetrate anything. All living organisms would be killed, but inanimate objects would remain intact. Ships would become aimless, meandering hulks; populated buildings would instantly become silent structures. Its line of sight was so sophisticated that it could pick out a single individual up to eight miles away. It could destroy a whole harbor's inhabitants by expanding the adjustable ray nozzle to various size openings and adjust the radiation level accordingly. With its captured radiation, the advantage was that nothing outside of the beam was contaminated or rendered harmful. A living organism touched by the beam would die from a massive overdose of concentrated radiation, reducing it to a small puddle of condensed steam.

The Americans intentionally allowed a rumor to leak out about the *Bronson*. It may have been just a trickle, but it was enough. After all, this was the Cold War, and the order of the day was to scare the living hell out of the other guys. This mere trickle, though, opened up the floodgates within the Communist world. With orders from the General Secretary, the Office of the KGB and Internal Affairs Office of the Kremlin had formed a special task unit of their most talented and cerebral individuals. Their assignment was to organize plans for the capture of the *Bronson* and her technology. A few select Party members knew the *Bronson* to be more than just rumor, and leaving their options open, let the decision that had been made go forward. The Communist leadership had no other alternative but to activate Russia's mole, and the USS *Bronson* would be his objective.

Friday, January 24, 1975 - 2130 hours

The nuclear carrier USS *John Preston*, a Kitty Hawk Class ship, carried with her 2,800 crew members, an additional 2,500 men from the five air wings out of North Island Naval Air Station, Marine aviators from Twenty-Nine Palms, and 72 Marines. Her after flight deck, starboard deck, and hangar bay were covered with diverse types of aircraft grouped in tight formation: F-14 Tomcats; A-6 Intruders; EA-6B Prowlers; F-4 Phantoms, and A-7 Crusaders. Four Navy E-2-C Hawkeyes were disbursed above and below deck, along with a variety of helicopters, including: CH-53 Sea Stallion Marine assault helos; SH-3G Sea King rescue choppers, and LAMPS' SH-2F ASW choppers. All these accounted for the 80 aircraft aboard the *Preston*.

Air crewmen and plane captains wandered through the rows to ensure the aircraft were ready for flight. With flight deck space as much at a premium as property in Malibu, aircraft wingtips were folded upward or arranged one over the other.

Making a visual inspection of the flight deck one last time from "Vulture's Row", Commander

Dean Morehouse, CAG (Commander of the Air Group), gulped down the last, cold mouthful of his second cup of coffee. He stepped back into the Roost, the cramped area jutting out of the superstructure on the port side, just aft of the bridge. It was from this vantage point that he, the Air Boss and Assistant Air Boss watched and directed launches and landings. He tossed his worn leather flight jacket over the arm of the swivel chair, then rolled down the neck of his yellow pullover jersey, the three inch black stenciled letters "CAG" visible across the back and chest.

"Colder than hell, huh, CAG?" Marty Whitney clattered his teeth together and grinned. On his first cruise as Assistant Air Boss, Whitney still proudly displayed his yellow jersey with the words 'Li'l Boss.'

"Damn right, it is," Dean shivered, "colder than a witch's tit. Expect it's gonna be colder before daybreak."

The past three days the 'Siberian Express' had been blasting across the North Pacific, but luckily this night saw calm seas with little surface wind, which was uncharacteristic for the Pacific in January. But it was a good night for flying.

Morehouse glanced upward at a golden moon and partly cloudy sky. Reality told him the peacefulness around him was a facade--all was not well with the world.

"Another cup of coffee, Mr. Morehouse?" asked Navy Steward Mindina, as he held up the Wardroom's sterling silver coffeepot. Mindina was noted for being the most meticulous steward ever stationed aboard the *Preston*. His white uniform jacket was always impeccable. Most of his lessons came early on in life. Growing up in Manila with a household filled with nine children, he being the oldest, his mother and father ensured that all of them were prepared for life.

"Thanks, Edward," CAG smiled as he held out his white ceramic cup. The steam from the hot coffee briefly fogged up his steel-rimmed glasses as he took a sip of the hot brew. The natural oil from the beans floated on the surface of the dark brown liquid, and he stared into the cup. "Good stuff, Edward," he chuckled as he turned away, mumbling to himself, "That's some ass-kickin' shit!"

Morehouse walked forward to the bridge, glancing at the Air Boss Captain (Select) Craig Dodson, who was being his usual, jittery self. Morehouse smiled. Dodson was acting more and more like a grandmother nervously watching over grandchildren left in her care. As Air Boss he was the key safety officer, the flight controller, ultimately having final responsibility for the launching and receiving of all aircraft. One sleeve of Dodson's yellow jersey was pushed up to his elbow, revealing a white grease pencil tucked under the stainless steel band of his Rolex.

CAG admitted it was times like these when he felt the same nervousness. With just the sheer number of men and aircraft, the experienced sailor knew that the likelihood of an accident was probable, loss of life likely. Every ninety seconds a plane is launched off each of the four cats. In the blink of an eye, it would only take one mistake, oversight, or a moment of carelessness, and a life would be snuffed out. A careless sailor, not paying attention, would end up 'hamburger meat' in the intake of a jet aircraft or blown over the side by powerful engine blasts. The strong current surging against this 1,000 foot vessel, all but assured certain death.

And to pilots flying at 10,000 feet, a four-acre, rolling, pitching flight deck looks like a postage stamp. The odds of an accident increases during night traps, as pilots lose their visual references because of their inability to see the horizon or the ocean. The only visible lights are tiny white lights, recessed in the deck and spaced apart every eight feet, lighting up the center of the landing area, with yellow lights running down each side. Pilots can only see the lights once they approached the carrier from the fantail. A miscalculation can send a multi-million dollar jet aircraft careening into the fantail, or "ass end" in Navy talk.

Morehouse sipped at his coffee as he returned to the Roost. Tapping his grease pencil against the window, he looked toward the horizon, waiting for any sign. That corner of the glass was clean now, all previous black marks removed, marks that helped him keep track of the earlier flights; he knew the exact position of his 'birds', the F-14 Tomcats. He thought about all the planes, all the flights he'd been associated with. There was pride and satisfaction knowing that he never lost a plane or crew member since reporting for duty aboard the *Preston* a year and a half ago. Four months of the cruise were already gone. He couldn't believe his tour was almost over, and in Navy terms, that meant he was getting short.

He remembered another carrier, four years earlier, when planes and men were lost daily, never to return from Southeast Asia. His recollections of that time brought back feelings of failure. He failed at his job, failed his men, unable to bring all of them home. Four years seemed like a lifetime ago.

Now, he was 2,400 miles from the waters off Vietnam and cruising fifty miles off the northeast coast of Japan, waiting for final orders that would send the fleet into the Sea of Japan. This time, instead of fighting in a war, the Navy was trying to prevent what could turn out to be a nuclear holocaust. The tension associated with the crisis was impossible to ignore, as it touched every man in the task force in one way or other.

Snapping to attention, a boatswain's mate announced the Captain's arrival. "Captain's on the bridge, sir!"

Captain Mike Donovan nodded, "Gentlemen." Donovan's Marine escort followed closely behind, immediately taking his position next to the door, standing at attention.

CAG turned and walked back onto the bridge. "Evening, Captain." Air Boss Dodson nodded with his typical unsmiling fashion, "Captain." He resumed his pacing.

Mike Donovan glanced at the stocky-framed Air Boss, thinking back when he held that same position and how much he had despised the ulcerous assignment. Yet, here he was with his first command of a carrier. The only other person on the carrier that was senior to him was Admiral Stanton Hewlett, whose only assignment was to ensure the task force completed its mission. It was Admiral Hewlett's flag the carrier was flying on this cruise.

Donovan was responsible for several air wings and twenty or more ships assigned to the task force. Cruisers, destroyers, supply ships made up part of the armada, disbursed sometimes up to hundreds of miles away from the carrier. Others stayed close by, leading, following and surrounding the *Preston*. They were there on an individual, and an integrated mission.

Donovan slid his hands into his back pockets. "How are things going, Craig? All the 'birds' back on deck?"

"Not yet, sir," answered the Air Boss. "Still have four 'felines' making their way in. CIC (Combat Information Center) reported them about 100 miles out. We should have them on the approach radar any time now."

Donovan walked over to the high-backed captain's chair, swiveling it back and forth. His authoritative voice suddenly boomed: "Everyone on station, Mr. Crawley?"

OOD (Officer of the Deck) Lieutenant Frank Crawley answered Donovan with quick precision as to the nautical "where-at" of each vessel. "Just need to check on the tanker, sir."

"Very well."

Crawley stepped outside the bridge, going to the starboard polaris used to take a ship's bearings in relation to the carrier. Making a notation, he came back to the quartermaster's station on the bridge. As he scanned his report, he unconsciously rubbed the bump on the bridge of his nose. In the Wardroom his fellow officers kiddingly called him 'Speedbump'.

"Captain, all vessels have correctly taken their stations."

Donovan nodded as he hiked up his khaki trousers, his protruding stomach more prominent lately. His sweet tooth just kept pushing him to too many desserts. "Excellent dinner tonight, Edward!"

"Thank you, Captain," Edward Mindina answered proudly.

Donovan turned toward XO Masters. "I noticed your plate was wiped clean, XO!"

"Yes, sir. We're lucky to have Edward with us," Executive Officer Masters smiled.

Wayne Masters and Mike Donovan served together previously aboard the Kitty Hawk during the Vietnam conflict. It was a known fact among the officers that the two had their differences, especially when it came to disciplinary action with the crew. Donovan's hard-line attitude didn't set well with Masters, even though he admitted to his fellow officers that there were very few problems among the men. He folded his arms across his chest, watching out of the corner of his eye as Donovan wandered over to the radar repeater.

The Captain's total concentration was on the screen as he eyeballed the green blips and checked his vector board. "Where's that pain in the ass trawler?" he barked softly.

"There it is, skipper, right there." Radarman Second Class Jack Summers rested his elbow on the lip of the table, tapping his grease pen on the screen. He gave a sideways glance at Donovan and frowned, his dark eyebrows resembling thick pieces of rope being drawn together by block and tackle. "But something's weird, sir."

"What's weird, 'Scopes'?" Donovan asked as he leaned closer to the screen, resting his hand on the countertop.

The young radarman avoided glancing at the twisted little finger on Donovan's right hand, a constant reminder of a returning flight to Cecil Field in Florida, when the landing gear of his Phantom collapsed. "Well, sir, he's been movin' around a lot the past couple of hours, never staying on the same course." Summers traced a route on the screen with his pen. "First he was at two seven zero degrees, now he's come around to starboard, heading one four five degrees." He went quiet for a second, then shook his finger in the air, a logical explanation popping into his mind. "Ya know, sir, I bet they're keeping tabs on the *Bronson* now that she's joined us." He pointed to the screen, "And there's the *Bronson*, sir. Expect they've lost their interest in us."

Russian trawlers were a common sight, always 'dogging' the American fleet, prowling the waters. Sporting huge quarter length Marconi-type antennas and other intercept designed military-type antennas, radar, and communication gear, they electronically 'eavesdropped' on the Americans and filmed their flight ops. They still didn't have a carrier--they wanted one.

"Tomcats are coming in from the west, sir," the Air Boss reported.

Leaning toward Radarman Summers, Donovan remarked, "Keep an eye on them, 'Scopes'." He patted Summers on the shoulder, his way of showing confidence in the young petty officer. Summers was good, able to juggle an entire task force.

Donovan went over near the Air Boss, leaning toward the window, scanning the water. "Has the Sea King lifted off?" The rescue chopper was always the first aircraft to leave the deck before flight ops ever began and hovered close by till the last plane was launched or returned.

"Yes, sir," Dodson answered, pointing in the direction of the angle deck before he walked back to the Roost.

A Grumman F-14 Tomcat, its landing lights in view, rode the wind rushing beneath its outstretched wings, the fighter resembling a majestic bald eagle floating on the air currents above the Rockies. Inside the cockpit, with one hand on the throttle and the other on the flight stick, the pilot gingerly maneuvered his aircraft, lining it up with the ship.

The pilot, Lieutenant William Fitzsimmons, checked in with the LSO (Landing Safety Officer) then checked his gauges and called in his name, speed and fuel weight. The tension on the arresting wires were immediately adjusted, set to match the weight and speed of the Tomcat.

The arresting wires were forty feet apart, but 'Wired Willy' had a special knack for always catching the number four wire, the last wire. The farthest from the fantail, number four was the pilot's final shot at a safe capture. Missing it meant he'd have to bolter, in other words, hit the afterburners and hope there was still enough deck in front of him. Bets were on throughout the ship. CAG Morehouse had been unsuccessful in curtailing the bets or Willy's number four wire capture.

With full power on, Fitzsimmons' 61,000 pound, missile-laden aircraft slammed onto the deck, his tailhook catching number four wire. But as nerve-wracking as Willy's landings were, he'd never once been given a 'wave off' or missed number four wire.

The arresting wire slithered backward along the deck, recoiling like a massive anaconda, until again stretched tightly, port and starboard sides. The four arresting wires waited for their next capture, and every forty-five seconds, they could expect another.

Edwards Air Force Base, California
January 25 - 1900 hours

A black, delta-winged aircraft, its two turbo-ramjet engines spewing orange flames, accelerated down Runway 19. Disappearing into a torrent of pelting rain, the giant 'bird' rose from the earth, pulling effortlessly away from gravity, its afterburners turning white hot. Reaching 25,000 feet, the aircraft immediately linked up with a tanker for in-flight refueling. Since the outer shell was made of titanium, it expanded under extremely high temperatures during flight. The fuel tanks were designed so they would leak until the aircraft was airborne, and then they would continue to expand until completely sealed. Because of this, the fuel was nearly expended by the time the aircraft was airborne.

With refueling completed, the fastest manned, highest flying reconnaissance plane, the SR-71 Blackbird reached farther into the heavens. Within minutes, it was cruising at 2,000 mph, at an altitude of nearly 72,000 feet. This multi-million dollar aircraft, equipped only with a sophisticated camera, radar and infrared systems, feared no one or nothing. Missiles or guns for self-defense were a mute issue. The 'Bird' was designed specifically to fly extremely high and with blinding speed. Even anti-aircraft missiles were useless against it, as witnessed by pilots during the Vietnam conflict. They reported seeing Soviet-made SAM2 missiles being fired at the Blackbird, but being unable to reach the altitude, they ultimately "fell from wends they came."

Sitting in the forward pilot's seat was Air Force Colonel Greg Dumont, with Captain David McMillans, Reconnaissance Systems Officer occupying the rear seat. Looking more like astronauts than pilots, both men were dressed in pressure suits and connected to life support systems. Their present mission, CIA authorized, would take them on a high-speed flyover of the China and North Korea borders. With their speed and altitude, it was possible for them to photograph 100,000 square miles in just one sixty-minute flyover. But today, they'd only need eight minutes to get the pictures requested.

Colonel Dumont put a last minute trim on the flaps and touched up the throttles to make the cruising speed and altitude. He adjusted the oxygen mask. "Dave, we have the latest weather out of Travis?"

"Yes, sir. It looks smooth all the way to Elmendorf."

"Great. Keep an eye out for the weather link off Seattle." Dumont checked his geographic display for positioning and corrected for a freak forty knot jet stream. He checked both panel displays located just forward of his knees and settled back to log his observations after putting the Bird on 'George', the auto pilot. "We're on 'George', Dave...hands off."

"Roger, skipper."

They flew silently for several minutes, which wasn't unusual. There was plenty to do when the Blackbird was up. But they'd flown many missions together in the SR-71, and after a while, one seemed to know what the other was thinking. McMillans smiled when he heard Dumont's voice in his headset.

"It'll get better over the water, Dave. We've just got the radar checkpoint in Adak, and then--"

McMillans continued making his notes and calculations as he finished the sentence, "...we're outta here!"

Pentagon
Sunday, January 26 - 1040 hours

Secretary of Defense Thomas Allington pointed to the aide, motioning for him to open the double doors then said, "Come in, Commander, Agent Phillips," he motioned, then with a condescending glance, said to his aide, "I'll be awhile." The aide immediately left. The solid wooden doors were securely closed, and a Marine guard, with a Smith & Wesson .45 strapped to his side, moved to take his position directly in front of them.

Allington assumed the role of Secretary of Defense with the election of President Samuel McNeely and Vice President Harold Shurmann in 1972. A twenty-year Navy veteran, Allington was assigned to the Judge Advocate General's Office the last six years of his military service, after which he began his own law practice. He began loosening his tie and stared at the uniformed men. "Gentlemen, you might as well get comfortable. Today has 'long day' written all over it."

Seated at the long, rectangular, mahogany table were four military officers making up the Joint Chiefs of Staff. The military brass shifted in their seats, brief smiles acknowledging the SecDef's remark. That's as comfortable as they would get. The austere military traditions of all the Armed Forces just didn't provide for a "time for loosening one's tie."

Four-star Army General Allan Sherwood, Chairman of the JCS, was the embodiment of a military officer who had learned early the lessons of the power of manipulation and the term "sucking up." For nearly thirty years, every move he made was meant to feed his ego and setting his goal and career path to becoming the youngest Chairman of the Joint Chiefs. He turned the normally placid meetings into the proverbial circus. The inside joke was that before anyone entered the room, they first threw in a thermometer just to check the temperature.

General Victor Norwood, USAF, Chief of Staff, had come to the Joint Chiefs directly from his assignment as head of the Strategic Air Command (SAC). Norwood was one of the first to fly the new B52A's delivered to the Air Force in 1954, and in 1959, he was part of NASA's X15 project, carrying the X15A beneath the B52's underbelly. He possessed the insight and judicious reasoning that would safeguard the aircraft from being replaced by newer bombers.

Admiral Carl Maxwell, USN, Chief of Naval Operations (CNO) and JCS Vice Chairman, had the most time-in service of all the Joint Chiefs. He, like Gene Morelli, had come up through the ranks. He had been a troubled sailor during the early part of his career, having gone through two marriages in less than six years, and known for his confrontations with the Shore Patrol on numerous occasions. Maxwell learned that drinking wasn't the way to win friends and influence people. So when he cleaned up his act and reached deep down inside himself to set a new course for his life, it guided him down a path to become CNO. Knowing both sides of the fence had made him a sailor's sailor. Even during the sad times of dishing out punishment to sailors, he was lenient and was jokingly, but fondly referred to as "Brother Maxwell" because of his sermons to the wayward sailors he had chastised.

General Orvis Black, USMC, Commandant of the Marine Corps, was a man of impeccable integrity and deep-reaching faith. With his clear blue eyes and close-cropped silver butch haircut, he was a Marine poster just waiting to be printed. During Vietnam, Black was Commanding General of the 5th Marine Division for I Corps in DaNang. Along with a Silver Star and Purple Heart that he earned during Korea, Black received the Distinguished Service Medal for cleaning up the northern cities of Hue and Phu Loc during the Tet Offensive. His loyalty to his men propelled him through the ranks, twice being deep selected in rank. In six months, General Black is scheduled to retire from the Marine Corps.

The Secretary nodded in the direction of Grant Stevens and Sam Phillips. "As you all know, Agent Phillips is representing the CIA, and Commander Stevens is here from NIS at the recommendation of Admiral Morelli."

"Big goddamn deal," General Sherwood muttered without turning around, rapping the tip of his pen on the table.

For the moment, almost everyone ignored the sarcastic remark made by the Chairman, that is, everyone but Grant. Sherwood hadn't changed. He drilled his stare into the back of the Chairman's head, a head that seemed balanced somewhat precariously on what Grant once described to Morelli as a "grizzled turkey neck."

The SecDef gestured toward the two-page agenda resting on the manila folders set before each of them. "You've had an opportunity to review the documents in front of you. Let's discuss the situation. General Norwood, do you have anything to report?"

Norwood pushed his chair back then walked somewhat tentatively to the map projected onto the screen. It was obvious the arthritis in his left hip was acting up, his limp more prominent. He looked up at the map. "Our first flyover by satellite shows the Chicom massing, right about here in

Ji'an and here, Dandong." He circled the two areas with a black-tipped wooden pointer. "About three hours after the satellite's pass, we had the Blackbird shoot the photos you have in your folders."

The 'Bird' did good work again, Grant thought, as he shuffled through the series of glossy, black and white photos.

"Analysis confirms those two sites," Norwood said as he tapped the screen, "and Nampo, right here on the northeast coast of North Korea. Each has missile launchers in position." He hesitated momentarily, looking up at the details of the map before he turned around, tapping the pointer against his palm. "All the missiles have been confirmed as launch-ready, with more stockpiled at each site."

"Are you planning more flyovers?" asked the Secretary as he lit another Marlboro, then went into a coughing fit, holding his handkerchief in front of his mouth, trying to muffle the disturbing sound.

Norwood replaced the pointer in the tray then returned to his chair. Looking at his watch, he answered, "The satellite should be making another pass as we speak."

Grant sat quietly in the background, absorbing every word, instinctively calculating and planning, compiling a mental list of questions and options that would decide life or death, perhaps his own. Every now and then he'd glance at the display that pinpointed every ship in the task force sailing off the northeast coast of Japan.

"We got a report from the long-range recon SEAL team, Tango Alpha, out of Japan," piped up the CNO.

Grant's attention immediately turned to the Admiral, even more so when hearing that the SEALs were involved, although, he would have been more surprised if they weren't. They were usually the first ones in. They were the Navy's 'silent option', a phrase coined by Stubby Brooks. SEAL Team 2 adopted it as their motto. Without thinking, Grant touched the 'Budweiser' above the rows of ribbons on his service dress blues jacket. Until that moment, he didn't realize how much he missed it, missed the Teams. Being stationed in D.C. and involved in intel activities kept him sharp, sensitized. But it just wasn't the same as being part of an operational team.

Admiral Maxwell ran a hand over the top of his balding head, then leaned on the edge of the table as he said, "The SEALs did a show and tell when they got back and reported seeing stacks of mortar rounds at the site in North Korea. Hell, they even got close enough to read the printing on the casings!" he said, his boastful tone unmistakable. "But this is where it gets baffling. According to the SEALs, the Chinese symbol on those mortars indicates they're only exercise rounds. I called WARCOM (Special Warfare Command for SEAL teams) in San Diego just to confirm that point after reading the Team's dance cards." He looked at each attentive face staring back at him before adding, "None of them are loaded with live ammo." He looked to his left, staring directly at Grant as he spoke those words, waiting for a reaction. Then he spotted something in Grant's eyes, the expression on his face revealing he already had an idea. "Your thoughts, Commander, can you add something at this point?"

Grant nodded, then stood by his chair, laying the folder and photos on the seat. "Sir, what if this isn't a plan to attack, or even to invade Korea at all? It has all the earmarks of the Patton diversion used in England, Admiral, when they planted dummy materials and troop movement."

Gene was right about this kid, thought the CNO, as he leaned back, intrigued, waiting to hear more.

The Secretary pulverized his cigarette in the ashtray, dropping it next to several extinguished butts, a thin haze of smoke hovering above the table. "Go on, Commander."

Grant rubbed the back of his neck as he formulated his thoughts. All eyes were on him while he slowly walked over toward the viewing screen in the corner of the room. Minute particles of dust seemed suspended within the projector's light beam. He broke the beam as he passed in front of it, a portion of the map visible on the back of his dark uniform jacket.

He glanced up at the map before turning to look at the Joint Chiefs and SecDef. "The report on this by the CIA points out the traffic they've intercepted between Russia and China has mentioned the USS *Bronson*. Suppose this is just some type of subterfuge, designed specifically to...?"

Chairman Sherwood wasn't about to wait for an explanation. With nostrils flaring, and a beet red face, he tore into Grant. "What the hell are you talking about? Subterfuge? You think this is some kind of goddamn game, Stevens?" The redness in his face slowly crept upward like the infamous Red Tide, plainly showing through his thinning gray hair.

Without even blinking, Grant answered the Chairman calmly. "No, sir. I can assure you I'm well aware this isn't a game. I've spent my career separating the authentic from the fraudulent...sir."

Admiral Maxwell didn't even attempt to hide his amusement, impressed that Grant wasn't rattled by the outburst and had even managed to politely 'slap back.' The other Joint Chiefs had grown accustomed to seeing this from the Chairman. Maxwell wished he could give Commander Stevens a 'thumb's up' sign, and with a tight smile, drilled his stare right through the angered Sherwood.

No love had been lost between these two, Sherwood and Maxwell. They had served together on the JCS for nearly three and a half years of their four-year appointment, always going head-to-head about every point of interest that approached the JCS offices. He turned back to Grant. "Proceed, Commander."

"Yes, sir. As I was saying, suppose this was

designed specifically to draw in the *Bronson*?" Grant's shadow projected against the screen as he reached up and traced his finger along the outline of the map. "Here we have the coast of Russia, North Korea and the Chinese border..." He repeatedly jabbed his index finger against the screen, pointing to an area east of Japan, then he intentionally stared at the red-faced Chairman. "And here we have the USS *Bronson*." Making eye contact with each of the Joint Chiefs and the SecDef, he continued: "It isn't just the *Bronson*, sirs; it's the microchip for the SNAGS we have to be concerned about. One chip in the hands of the Russians, then one chip is duplicated, and then the Chinese have it. The Free World could be brought to its knees. I submit to you that the Korean scenario is a ruse, and the *Bronson* is their true target."

General Black got up and walked to the double doors, eyeing the Marine sergeant's impeccable uniform, but not really examining it. He turned and stared at Grant. "We all know about the SNAGS, Commander, and what would happen if it fell into the wrong hands."

Grant cleared his throat. One quick look at CNO Maxwell's expression reinforced the fact that he got carried away trying to get an unnecessary point across.

Black stood behind his chair, resting his hands on the leather back, as he said, "What we want to know is if you have anything at all to substantiate what you're implying?"

"No, sir, I don't," answered Grant, "but the coincidence is too great. Our intel, along with the CIA's, reported that the Russians have known there was more to the *Bronson* than what's already been leaked. We know how badly they want what's on board, and it's becoming apparent they're willing to do anything to get it."

Agent Phillips nodded, then stood slowly, everyone shifting their eyes to him. "The Commander seems to reflect my feelings, gentlemen, and according to the bits of information from our radio intercept stations at Adak and Kamisaya, it appears that Korea is the Commander's 'Patton.'"

"So, why get the Chinese involved?" asked Allington as he rubbed his reddened eyes. "Why aren't the Russians just running the show themselves and trying to take it all?"

Grant walked over to the end of the table, grinding his fist into his palm. "My guess is they knew we'd go all out to protect Korea by sending our best. What better way to fire us up then to get China involved, too? And with the technology that's at stake, I'm sure the Chicoms were anxious to be willing participants."

The CNO swung his chair around, folding his arms across his barrel chest. "Commander Stevens, let's assume your theory is correct. How do you propose they would go about getting their hands on this technology? We've got a whole damn fleet out there with the *Bronson*, not to mention the *Bronson* herself."

"Right now, Admiral, I honestly don't know what

their plan is. But my first guess is that they're counting on us not to unleash anything until they make the first decisive move, if they make a move at all, sir. And..." Grant took a deep breath, knowing the reaction his statement was going to receive, "I believe that this will all come about with the assistance of a Russian mole."

"What! Are you out of your freakin' mind?" shouted Allan Sherwood as he flew out his chair.

Allington had had all he could take and brought his fist down hard on the table. "For Christ's sake, Allan!" His voice tore through the room as he pointed at Sherwood. "Sit down before you have a goddamn heart attack!" He didn't take his eyes from the Chairman until Sherwood was settled in his seat, then he turned back to Grant. "Go on, Commander." He gave Sherwood a quick glance.

"Yes, sir. The CIA and NIS have suspected for a long time that there was a mole somewhere in our military, in the Navy more specifically. What better time for him to surface?"

Admiral Maxwell pushed his chair back then got up and walked toward Grant. Even though he was a few inches shorter than the younger officer, his very presence could be intimidating, with eight rows of ribbons, piercing brown eyes, and a commanding attitude. That is, intimidating to anyone else but Grant, who was always respectful, but never intimidated. Maxwell rested his hands on his hips, rocking back and forth on his heels, staring down at his highly polished black Navy shoes, and mulling over what had just been put on the table. Finally looking up at Grant through narrowed eyes, he asked, "Commander Stevens, do you have any opinion as to when they'll try to carry this out?"

Grant paused a moment before responding. "I suspect the time is getting closer, Admiral, especially with the reports and photos showing the troops and missiles in the positions they're in. There's not much left for them to do." He slapped the back of his hand into his palm. "Look, they made their threats against South Korea knowing we'd send a fleet to protect it. They counted on us sending the *Bronson*. They've had a little more than three months to finalize their plans, and they got their troops and artillery into position faster than hell." The right side of his mouth curved up. "But I guess they didn't count on a SEAL team taking a sneaky peak, Admiral."

Maxwell nodded approvingly, a hint of a smile appearing. "I have another question, Commander. Wouldn't it be prudent for us to confront them now, tell them about the exercise rounds, in other words, call their bluff?"

Grant shook his head. "The exercise rounds only affect the mortars, sir, not the missiles, and they've got a helluva lot of troops out there."

Maxwell glanced at the SecDef then back at Grant. "And...?"

"While you were negotiating, you could be giving them the time they needed to go for the *Bronson*. I believe we need to move forward and prevent it from happening, and hopefully, uncover the mole." Maxwell detected the concern showing in Grant's eyes. "I know that's an extreme risk, Admiral, but one I feel we've got to consider taking. And getting back to your earlier question, sir, as far as how they plan on carrying it out, I don't know, sir, at least...not yet. But I do have an idea on how we can find out, sir," he said with a broad grin.

Maxwell saw the look, the excitement in the eyes of Grant Stevens, and he smiled inwardly, wishing he still possessed that same enthusiasm. He shook his head and smiled, saying over his shoulder as he went back to his chair, "Somehow, I thought you might, Commander. I thought you just might."

CHAPTER THREE

Kodiak, Alaska

The First National Bank of Kodiak had been erected on the corner of Birch Avenue and Mill Bay Road during the latter half of 1972. The two-story building drew few curiosity seekers during the nine months of construction. After all, it was just another bank, the second one in town. For the grand opening the amiable employees handed out free ball-point pens and calendars with a colored photograph of the bank displayed across the top half. A massive, high-luster steel door to the vault was kept open the first two days, prospective customers allowed to see into the vault itself. Beyond the main door was a second door made up of 3-1/2" diameter steel bars, the bars acting as another security feature. Most impressive for such a small town bank, the residents remarked.

Adjacent to the rear of the bank, facing Baranof Street, were two shops, one sold hunting and fishing supplies, and the other, dry goods. Above the shops, two small, two bedroom apartments had been built. The kitchenettes were completely stocked, living rooms and bedrooms fully furnished. Each apartment had its own access, one wooden staircase on Baranof, and one in the alleyway. The shops and apartments were designed around a steel-encased elevator shaft, built behind false walls, in between the bank and the building. A recessed roof covered the top of the building. Hidden beneath were satellite communications dishes, out of site from prying eyes.

The inhabitants of Kodiak were unaware that more than just routine activities were carried out at the First National Bank and the shops. All employees were either CIA or U.S. Navy officers, because buried four levels below the bank structure, a highly classified, sophisticated Computer Center was located in small-town Kodiak, Alaska. The center looked like something from a Star Trek episode, with its rows of computer screens blinking and scrolling unrecognizable alien language. A green, neon-like glow from the monitors filled the room and gave the operators an unearthly pallor, as the lights brightened, dimmed and flickered on their faces. Four printers, lined up on the north wall, clattered like typewriters gone berserk. Reams of paper lay in the trays behind them, with a paper shredder close by.

Every component of the *Bronson's* equipment, every missile, the guidance system, navigation, and radar were entirely controlled by its 'brain', the Tactical Support Computer (TSC) MK1 system. From the moment it was brought on-line, the TSC-MK1 computer had performed impeccably, pumping information to the three terminals, spewing out vital details at a moment's notice. Every movement the ship made was controlled by the TSC.

Nothing escaped it. Images picked up by the ship's radar were instantly transformed on the screens at Kodiak. The very heartbeat of the *Bronson* was recognized, explained and detailed on computer printouts. The Center was the very 'lifeblood' of the USS *Bronson*. All commands were encrypted instantaneously, sent to one of two satellites, then unencrypted when picked up by the ship's computer, the same process when coming back to Kodiak. CIA Headquarters in Langley, Virginia, received enciphered, thorough reports--Command Center data, *Bronson* data--passed constantly, over and over. Not a command was issued of which Langley wasn't aware.

Three mini-cameras were positioned inside a protective shield running along the outside top edge of the ship's bridge. Camera 1 was aimed across the bow of the ship, Camera 2 down the port side, and Camera 3 down the starboard side, all capable of turning from 0 to 180 degrees. Cameras 2 and 3 were responsible for images off the stern. Live broadcasts were sent from the *Bronson* to the center. Color television monitors, three for each terminal, were individually set in built-in shelves just above eye level. Langley received simultaneous broadcasts, seeing the same picture as Kodiak.

Precautionary measures had been taken by setting up three backup sites, exact replicas of Kodiak. They were located in Scotland, Morocco, and Australia. Each site had a sector to control, allowing the *Bronson* a world-wide range and backups to boot.

The Computer Center was powered by its own generator, including a UPS (Uninterruptable Power Source) for 30 minutes of emergency power, giving the Kodiak site time to switch to a backup site, each of the three on standby, 24 hours a day. The room was 2,000 square feet, built on raised flooring, made up of individual panels, like three-foot square ceiling tiles, some dotted with small holes. Cold air, shooting upward through the openings, made the room a comfortable 68 degrees, which was critical to the hardware's operation.

Beneath the flooring lay a crawl space, two feet in height, running the length and width of the room. In the space was a jumble of cables, a snake pit of green, yellow, blue and red cabling wire, tagged with neatly inscribed labels. Each cable, about an inch in diameter, was composed of many smaller wires, multiple connections for each piece of computer hardware to which it was assigned. Thirty miles of cables sat beneath the floor, sending electronic pulses at half a million bytes per second, fast enough to send an entire library's data in a matter of hours.

All of the keyboards were designed to register and recognize the fingerprints of the naval officers authorized to control the SNAGS. If, at any time security was breached and the center was about to fall under the physical control of an adversary, small explosive charges were strategically distributed within the walls, floor and inside the computer itself. They were automatically set to go off when anyone other than the men assigned even touched the computer system. An emergency tunnel was easily accessible if the normal exit was blocked. Beneath a section of the floor, where the cables had been rerouted, the tunnel was made of steel and waterproof, leading to the basement of the dry goods shop.

Seven Navy officers, considered to be tops in their fields, had been selected from a list of mathematicians and computer engineers. Each required White House security clearance. They were between the ages of 22 and 33, unmarried, and none had personal responsibilities that could interfere with their demanding assignment. They wore civilian clothes, on and off duty, and carried Social Security Cards and civilian driver's licenses under assumed names. When they weren't on duty, they melded into the civilian community as bank and shop employees. They always stayed within range of their special locating devices, similar to beepers, carried at all times in case of an emergency and there was a recall to the center. However, these devices were installed inside wrist watches, pulsing silently when a signal was received.

A duty roster was instituted to rotate three of the officers every eight-hours. Any longer and it would be counter-productive. There was always the fear that a mistake could ultimately cause a catastrophic event involving the *Bronson* or the crew in Kodiak; attention to detail was critical.

Eight heavily armed Marines were assigned as

security, rotating watches every six hours. When four had completed a 24-hour rotation, they were off the next day in the rotation and the other four took over. They were posted within the 12" thick steel doors, a .45 holstered on their web belts and carrying an M-16 with six clips of 20 rounds. Even though they weren't required to stand at attention during their watches, they were well aware of the criticality of their assignment. Being Marines, one could usually find them at a 'stiff' parade rest.

Computer Room, Kodiak

Lieutenant Commander Jeff Holland sat at the keyboard watching the monitor. He and Lieutenant Commander Bob Little shared responsibility as Operations Officers, in charge overall for surface navigation, guidance, weapons control and interpretation of diagnostics. Holland had just settled into his watch, having just relieved Little. He sat at the keyboard as the TSC-MK1 processed millions of bytes of data. For the amount of data processing, the idle time still showed at 90%. "Jesus, this thing still amazes me," he mumbled. He glanced at the three monitors, checked the radar screen, then at precisely 2210 hours he typed in the command for the *Bronson* to reduce her speed to ten knots. He hit the 'enter' key. The response came back instantly. "Alllriightt! Let's keep playing, baby!" He sent the command for the ship to come left to 315 degrees. The *Bronson* responded immediately, heeling almost unnoticeably to starboard as she came about to her new course.

On board the destroyer, its only crew member was CIA Agent Tony Mullins, an ex-Navy UDT frogman. His background as a boatswain's mate, familiar with navigation, communications and gunnery was the basis of his qualifications to sit in the 'hot seat', as it was known. But most of the time he merely had to maintain communications with Langley and the Control Center at Kodiak. Mullins would joke that he was just along 'for the ride', when in all actuality, this man, living in solitude, was one of a handful trained to use the SNAGS system, the ultimate offensive/defensive weapon.

During the day at 1000 hours, then again at midnight, Mullins would assume control of the Bronson by flipping the override switch. Once again, encrypted codes were used to release the ship from Kodiak. For three hours he would test the integrity of the controls and gauges. After Kodiak resumed control, he would spend most hours secluded within the bowels of the destroyer, completing paperwork, recording in the log and communicating the day's events with Langley and Kodiak.

Surrounded by layers of reinforced steel, one entrance from above and one emergency escape route, he was secure in his habitat. The escape hatch would have to be used only as a desperation escape. Hanging alongside the hatch was a specially designed, Velcro-edged, wraparound wetsuit and air tank. The hatch opened to a pressurized chamber, giving him less than five seconds to prepare himself before being jettisoned beneath the ship once the watertight door was shut. And if he didn't have the time to shutdown the engines, he'd be fighting for his life in the churning turbulence under the ship. A predicted path would take him dangerously close to being sucked into the rotating screws.

Again, his past experience had helped land him the assignment. Mullins had been a combat swimmer instructor at the Navy Underwater Demolition School where UDT students were trained and prepared for the covert and riverine missions they would face. Mullins' nickname was "Legs". When his students were put on their backs for the flutter kick exercise to strengthen the abdomen and gluts and build endurance, it was odds on money that every student in class would be winded and spent before "Legs" Mullins even began to think about resting. He goaded new students with, "Remember, ladies...the only easy day was yesterday!" Mullins could swim the seven mile ocean course required for students, and would never use his arms. It was spooky. Yet, he would finish first, even as a student. He and other instructors pushed their students beyond what any student thought was physically and mentally possible of himself. The instructors were often heard to say: "It's mind over matter, gentlemen--if I don't mind, it doesn't matter!" If anyone could propel himself clear of the screws, "Legs" was the best bet going.

CHAPTER FOUR

Monday, January 27 - 0645 hours

During the night the SSN *Bluefin* set her course for one eight zero degrees, distancing herself from the carrier. She was a Sturgeon Class, Fast Attack Nuclear Sub built at the Mare Island Naval Shipyard in Vallejo, California, and commissioned in 1970. She was designed partially for reconnaissance, but mainly, she was built for speed. Her outer hull had few deck projections that interrupted the clean, streamlined form. Many of the masts had fairings on top of them to minimize turbulence when they were retracted. Powered by one water-cooled, pressurized nuclear reactor with one turbine, she carried onboard MK46 Astor nuclear and conventional torpedoes, and Harpoon anti-ship missiles. *Bluefin*'s immediate assignment, though, would have nothing to do with the launching of torpedoes or recon patrols. This silent hunter-killer was to play what seemed a very minor role in a very major production. She would set the stage for the *coup de grace* in a sophisticated plot designed to avoid nuclear war.

Hopping up onto the slightly raised periscope stand, the sub's captain issued the order at precisely 0635 hours. "Take her up! Bring her to periscope depth."

"Aye, aye, Captain," answered the OOD. He stood behind the helmsman and reached overhead, hanging on to the support bar. "Helm, five degrees up bubble. Make your depth sixty feet."

The helmsman locked his eyes on the gauges and dials in front of the wheel, watching the bubble displaying the angle of the boat. "Aye, aye, sir, up bubble. Passing 250 feet."

"Conn, we're passing 250 feet," the OOD notified the Captain.

After several minutes, the helmsman called out, "Passing 100 feet, sir...80 feet...we're at 60 feet, sir."

"Up periscope," the captain ordered. Hydraulics whined as the periscope rose. He draped his arms over the handles, rotating the periscope slowly. "There it is! One three five degrees. Down scope! OOD, make preparations to surface!"

"Aye, aye, sir. Make preparations to surface!" He immediately sounded the horn, the noise blaring throughout the boat. "Stand by to surface! Three degrees up bubble."

"Smitty, stand by the hatch!" COB (Chief of the Boat) ordered.

"At forty-five feet sir," the helmsman called out, his eyes still glued to the gauges and dials.

"Captain, the tower is clear," COB responded, walking closer to the ladder.

Grabbing the ladder's handrail, the captain called, "Mr. Reese, you've got the Conn. I'm going topside. C'mon, Chief!"

"Aye, aye, Captain," responded OOD Reese.

An immense, dark shape rose from the abyss, the attack sub settling on the ebony-colored water of the North Pacific. White, foamy, sea water spilled down the sail and over the black hull. Ocean spray washed across the deck, being carried by a strong northerly wind, bringing with it a threatening, rolling cloud cover and four foot swells. The sail hatch opened. At the top of the sail, twenty feet above the deck, the captain and chief scrambled out, binoculars raised, immediately searching the horizon.

"There it is!" the chief called out.

The helo pilot maneuvered his aircraft and headed for the *Bluefin*, struggling against a strong headwind. Sea King pilot, Lieutenant Troy McPherson spoke into the mini mike on his headset: "*Bluefin*, this is Sea King 6. Stand by for personnel transfer. Over."

"Roger, Sea King. Standing by," responded OOD Reese from the Conn. "Transfer personnel to the after hatch. Take your orders from Ground Control. Over."

"Roger, *Bluefin*." Lieutenant McPherson fought to hold the chopper steady, as it was buffeted by the bone-chilling wind. He centered it directly above the sub's after deck just forward of the escape hatch. The backwash from the helo's main rotor blades sprayed sea water over the men on deck. Crouching low, they continued engaging the whirlwind descending from above, as they battled a twenty knot wind.

Cupping his hands around his mouth, the Chief yelled down from the sail to ground control Petty Officer Smith, "Make sure you're grounded, Smitty! There's a lot of static charge there!" Smitty gave a thumb's up and pressed the headphones tighter against his ear.

The helo crew wouldn't have many chances to put their passenger on the submarine's deck--time wasn't in their favor with the rest of the fleet so close, and except for a handful of people, no one outside the sub's crew were privy to his presence. The motor whined as the wire cable began lowering its cargo.

Aboard the SSN *Bluefin*

COB Cal Davis, a Machinist Mate Master Chief, escorted Grant down narrow passageways, through watertight doors, and down ladders to 03 level. As Chief of the Boat, Davis' duties included being master-at-arms when disciplinary action was called for, and he acted as liaison between the CO and enlisted men. Davis was one of the most respected and trusted men aboard the *Bluefin*.

COB swung open the watertight door, and Grant stepped into the torpedo room just forward of midships. Davis followed him, putting the 'cocoon' down near one of the torpedoes. "Hope this is awright, sir," he said through an unmistakable Texas twang. "We were informed ya'd only need some temporary space, and the Captain said to stow ya here."

Grant laughed then gave the Master Chief and torpedoes a quick once-over. He'd seen it before; they all looked alike after a while. He replied with a smile, "This will do fine, Master Chief." Grant had noticed the broad back of his escort, reminding him of his football teammate at the Academy, defensive tackle Chuck Wyneski. "Say, did you ever play football?"

"No, sir, six years of boxing. In my younger days, I was Navy Golden Gloves, middleweight."

"Is that right? Sounds like you'd be somebody handy to have around!"

"Guess I can hold my own, sir," Davis laughed. He walked forward to the watertight door. "The Captain wants to see ya in his quarters after you've settled in, sir."

Grant walked aft and dropped his gear next to the bulkhead on the port side near one of the cocoons. "I'm ready now. Lead the way."

As he followed the red-headed Davis back up to the 01 level, Grant had a chance to briefly think about the flights that delivered him to the *Bluefin*. The F-14 Tomcat, with him sitting in the RIO's seat, took off from a runway at Patuxent Naval Air Station in Maryland at 1300 hours. It refueled in flight over Ohio and Washington State before landing at Elmendorf Air Force Base, Alaska, with an F-4 Phantom fueled and waiting for him on the runway. Somewhere over the North Pacific, the Phantom refueled with a KA-6D tanker from the USS *Ranger*. Within hours, the Phantom landed at Kyota Air Base in Japan. Grant barely had time to grab an apple and a cup of coffee before the air crewman hustled him off to the helo that would take him on the last leg of his journey. As the Sea King lifted from the tarmac, it rotated slowly to assume its new heading, its nose dipping as the pilot applied power. Grant looked out the window at the last bit of Mother Earth he'd be seeing for awhile.

"First time aboard a sub, sir?" asked Davis as they started back up to the 01 level.

"Not hardly, Master Chief, it's just that the air always seems a little...thick," he grinned as he slipped a finger inside the neck of his T-shirt, pulling it away from his throat. It was a strange world to be in, a sealed world for these submariners, one of work, sleep and eat, punctuated with an occasional card game. They shared one common enemy, though...the sea around them.

Davis laughed. "You'll get used to it, sir."

"No offense, COB, but I don't think I'll be hanging around long enough!"

Davis rapped his fist on the bulkhead next to the entrance of the stateroom on 01 level. The cabin was located just forward of the Sonar and Radio Room and the XO's stateroom. Hardly a stateroom one might find on a cruise ship, the cabin was barely 8 x10. The bunk was a foldaway unit, emphasizing the compactness of the cabin. "Captain, Commander Stevens is here," Davis announced.

A man who looked as if he should have been playing for the L.A. Lakers pushed the curtain aside and extended a large, black hand to Grant. "Commander. Welcome aboard the *Bluefin*," smiled Captain Reggie Stafford. A graduate of Princeton University, Stafford completed tours at SUBPAC in Hawaii, and Groton, Connecticut, and taught physics at the Naval Academy. He assumed command of the *Bluefin*'s Gold Crew in July, 1974. Each sub has at least two rotating crews assigned to it, a Gold and Blue crew, since seventy days is the max for any one crew to stay submerged.

"Glad to be here, sir," Grant replied.

A laugh from deep within Captain Stafford exploded in the small stateroom. "Are you sure about that? I've seen the orders, remember?"

Grant smiled. "Would you believe me if I told you my boss talked me into it?"

Stafford shook his head. "Morelli and I go back a long way, Grant. May I call you 'Grant'?"

"By all means, sir."

"As I was going to say, that wouldn't surprise me at all, except..." He stared at Grant through deep-set brown eyes, moving his ruler-length finger in a slow arc. "I've heard about you, Commander Stevens...oh, yes I have."

"Good or bad, sir?" Grant asked with a mischievous grin.

"I've heard about you and some of the stories behind those five rows of ribbons. Why don't we just leave it at that?" he laughed.

"Fair enough, Captain."

Rotating the combination lock, Stafford opened

the small safe above his desk and removed a large, brown envelope, its seal already broken. He withdrew the papers, and then turned slowly in his swivel chair to face Grant, scrutinizing Grant's chest ribbons and pins. Pointing at one pin in particular, he asked inquisitively, "Before we get down to business, answer me one question."

"Sir?"

"Well, I understand they call that SEAL pin a 'Budweiser.' Can you explain why, or would that be a breach of SEAL security?"

Grant shook his head and grinned. "No, sir, it's no secret. After graduation from BUD/S, new SEALs celebrate by ordering a round of Bud boilermakers, then they drop in the pins, drink till the glass is empty, and then catch the 'Budweiser' with their teeth. And it looks like the Bud emblem a little, don't you think, sir?"

Stafford laughed. "It certainly does! I guess this is just another fine tradition to be carried on in typical Navy fashion!"

He motioned to two seats attached to the bulkhead and separated by a table. "Now have a seat, and let's discuss these orders of yours." The two men sat at the desk, and Stafford noticed Grant's hands. There were old scars on the back of both hands. Stafford's immediate impression was they were very strong hands. "Are you into martial arts, Grant?"

Somewhat surprised by the sudden change in conversation and the Captain's astute observation, Grant rubbed his hands together as if trying to conceal secrets, then he responded, "I...I've been known to break a few...uh, shall we say, boards, sir." Maintaining a deadpan expression, he added, "Tried a piece of granite once, but it didn't work out. Now I only pick on Cool Whip and pillows."

Stafford roared again. As their eyes met, Stafford detected the moment as being uncomfortable for Grant, and he hastily changed the subject. "This operation is going to get a little dicey. Are you sure you can count on your contact being prepared? He better be squared away and ready for you. You've got to agree that timing is going to be everything on this one."

"Yes, sir, very true, but I know Joe Adler. I can vouch for him," he replied emphatically, "and I know I can depend on him throughout this assignment, sir. That's the way it has to be...for both of us."

"I see." Stafford's brow wrinkled as he centered his stare on Grant, thinking the younger officer a bit cocky. *Well, for the line of work he's in, maybe that's what it takes to survive the tough ones*. "I'm sure you're right, Grant," he said, nodding his head. "According to Morelli, you and this Adler have a working history."

"Yes, sir, we do," Grant answered simply.

Stafford knew it was time to get on to business. He placed the papers on the table. "Now, give me all the details."

The two officers sat in the stateroom for another hour, reviewing, calculating, and planning. They had fourteen hours to prepare, and nothing could be left to chance.

USS *Preston* - 1025 hours

Senior Chief Boatswain's Mate Joe Adler of the EOD team stepped into the EOD locker and slammed the steel vault-like door behind him. Lieutenant John Britley turned around from the desk. "Chief, how's it going topside?" Britley ran the tip of the eraser along the one inch scar above his right eyebrow, the result of his first wrestling match while a sophomore at the University of Wisconsin.

"No problems since Lieutenant Hall's Tomcat came in with the hung Phoenix, sir." Adler pushed up the sleeve of his red jersey, glancing at his watch. "Uh, sir, it's about time for--"

Britley dropped the pencil and shoved the chair back. "Say no more, Chief. I'll see if I can get into trouble topside." He smoothed back a lock of black hair from his forehead, and then grabbed his hat. "Report to the flight deck when you're through, Chief."

"Aye, aye, sir."

The EOD locker was located in the aft part of the hangar bay one level below the flight deck. It was one of the most secure areas on the carrier, save the nuclear storage magazines, which only Britley, his team and the Gunners Mate techs had access to. The security was necessary not only because of all their gear, but because of nuclear weapons documentation that required extra security. The notebooks and papers were stored in special metal trunks that only EOD Officer Lieutenant John Britley and Chief Adler had the combination for.

The 10 x 18 compartment had four bunk beds, along with a small 'head' and shower. The shower doubled as their personal "rain locker", and in case of decontamination, an emergency wash-down station, with a disposable drain where the water washed into sealable fifty-five gallon drums. But depending on which way the drain valve lever was pushed, the water could also flow into the ship's waste system. The locker was also equipped with dedicated electrical wiring with a battery powered lantern backup for emergencies. Should the carrier lose power, for any reason, the battery would kick in, lighting up the "battle" lanterns and keep the electronic combination vault door operable.

Considering the EOD team was only five to six men and could make an entire cruise with little or no attention paid to them--no inspections, no watches, and no shore duty--it was the perfect cover, with total seclusion whenever necessary. The team members had been told of Grant's plan. They'd be making themselves scarce, only using the locker during work hours, and only after Chief Adler had been informed. Within their tight-knit community, they didn't worry about leaks, their own line of work calling for total security, individual safety forcing them to depend on one another. The exhaustive security clearance procedures they had passed ensured their 'zipper' mouth demeanor. Besides, the special warfare camaraderie forbid throwing any team member under the bus for any reason. Whenever instructed on the importance of security measures, their standard, flip reply would be: "Don't worry...we're cleared for stupid and ridiculous."

Adler dropped his starched, green EOD hat, called a “barracks cover”, on the desk, then went to the sink and splashed some cold water on his face. Clear, soft blue eyes stared back at him from the mirror as he wiped the towel over his chin. His weathered face exhibited more creases and more lines these days, a far cry from the face of a sixteen year-old who'd run away from an orphanage in St. Paul to join the Navy. Twenty-two years he'd given Uncle Sam, the first fourteen as UDT, the last eight as EOD.

Stashed away in his brain were instructions for disarming every known type of ordnance in the world. Like his team members, it wasn't the known ordnance they feared, it was the so-called 'hippie bombs', IEDs, the unknowns. *How ironic,* he thought. *Here I am disarming bombs, and while I was UDT, I was blowing them up intentionally.* But it was these assignments and duties that cost him a marriage, the one regret of his long career. Otherwise, there wasn't a minute he would have changed. He smiled thinking about the bumper sticker on the rear of his red 1967 Mustang: EOD--WHAT A BLAST.

Putting on his MK6 transceiver headset, he adjusted the miniature mouth mike. The small unit would be powerful enough since his contact was only about a mile away from the carrier. He looked at his battered, matte gray Benrus diving watch. *Right on time...1030 hours.* He flipped the switch. "Adler here."

"How ya doing, Chief?"

"Good, sir." Adler could hear the smile in Grant's voice. They'd been through the shit and sticks together not all that long ago with the Libyan raids.

"Did you get the info?"

"Roger that, sir. Scheduled time is 2030 hours. I'll call and nail down a confirmation."

"Very well."

"I'll be lookin' for you, Panther." It'd been a long time since he had used the code name Grant once used in the field.

"Roger. See you tonight! Out."

Adler locked the door and said quietly, "This is gonna be good!" As he made his way across the hangar deck, an instant snapshot of a past incident flashed through his mind, causing him to remember his friend and how impressed he'd been with him during one of those raids in the Libyan desert. While he set the shaped charges on the terrorist training camp's ammo supply, Grant managed to hold off ten or twelve Libyans and then pulled a wounded British SAS operator out of the shit storm, carrying him 400 meters back to the LZ (Landing Zone).

Aboard the SSN *Bluefin*

Grant left the sub's Sonar and Radio Room, returning to the torpedo room on 03 level. He and the chief made a good team. Adler had one of the coolest heads and steadiest hands for anyone he'd ever seen around explosives. He had responded to Captain Stafford's question that he could count on his contact. There wasn't a doubt in his military mind. Joe Adler was as good as they came.

He pulled his luggage, known as “cocoons”, away from the bulkhead and knelt down to check everything one more time. The two black fiberglass, waterproof cocoons looked more like 250 pound bombs but weighed only 25 pounds each, and once in the water had neutral buoyancy. One held his clothes and weapons, the other his diving gear and the makings for a variety of IED's. Adler would provide whatever else he'd need from the EOD 'cookbook', depending on the type of IED required.

Throughout the rest of the day he stayed pretty much to himself, considering there weren't too many places a visitor could go on a submerged submarine. Shortly after lunch, he slipped on his Navy shorts and T-shirt and went to the port side, aft of the torpedo racks, carving out a small niche to use as his personal fitness center. Sweat poured from his face, his muscles ached. For 45 solid minutes, all out, non-stop, he pushed himself through his ritualistic sit-ups, pushups and flutterkicks. His breathing was deep, heavy, the acrid smell of oil and grease creeping into his senses. But he kept his mind focused on reviewing and formulating events for that evening and the time beyond that, when all his energy and intelligence would come into play. Few were aware of his assignment--millions would never know.

At 1815 hours he walked aft to the crew's mess. He already had an early light dinner in the cramped Wardroom with Stafford and his officers, but this would be just a snack to tide him over. He'd need the extra protein and carbohydrates because it was going to be a long evening, with his work cut out for him. It would take a lot of fuel for the body.

The crew's mess hall had many uses, not excluding emergency sickbay and auditorium. It was a gathering place for the enlisted men, to get the latest scuttlebutt, play cards, or just read. A mass of overhead fluorescent lights illuminated the room, in sharp contrast to the brown paneling covering the bulkheads. Various plaques and awards won by past and present crews were displayed throughout.

Heads turned when he walked in. An officer getting food in the enlisted mess? Creating a stir for the second time since he'd come aboard, Grant acknowledged the submariners with a nod and smile. His reason for coming aboard was pretty hush-hush, even the boat's Radioman, Sparky Johnson, known as the "1MC of scuttlebutt", hadn't a clue, at least that's what he claimed. The crew had only been informed they'd be receiving a passenger.

Other than that, the *Bluefin*'s orders were standard. They'd be going through the routine of firing solutions on the fleet that night, keeping in practice. And that much was correct, but there would be a slight interruption, a slight variation in the routine.

Grant grabbed a tray and started through the chow line, ordering a cold, turkey sandwich with extra white meat and mayo on whole wheat bread. He slid the food tray along the metal rack and reached for a plain baked potato, and a banana, not completely ripe. He took the last piece of apple pie, just because it looked good. The ice cubes "clinked" as they bounced against each other on the bottom of the glass, then he poured some "bug juice" from the juice machine. Watching the strawberry-colored liquid flowing into the clear plastic glass, he wondered who the hell came up with the name "bug juice" for Kool-Aid.

While he waited for his sandwich to be made, he spotted a copy of the latest issue of All Hands laying on one of the tables close to the end of the chow line. One side of the magazine was folded under, exposing an article that caught his eye. Very curious, he sat on the edge of the bench, reading the title "Fastest Ship in the Fleet". Immediately, he thought of the *Bronson* and her classified status. But it was just a review of the new Surface Effect Ship, a hydrofoil with speeds of over 75 knots that was being tested in Panama

City, Florida. On his way out of the mess hall, carrying his tray full of food, he felt the stares of the few remaining submariners sitting at the tables.

For ten minutes Grant waited alone in the sub's Radio Room, a headset hanging around his neck, one leg propped up against the wall. Sparkey Johnson was somewhat reluctant to turn the communication's gear over to him again and did so only after some reassurance from Master Chief Davis. Tossing the crumbled Snicker's candy wrapper into the trash, he finished the last mouthful of cold milk.

He glanced at his watch and slipped the headset on, just as the signal came at precisely 2030 hours. "Whatcha got going, Joe?"

Chief Adler's voice came in clear, his message brief. "Sir, flight ops have ended. This might be a good time for you to lock-out."

"I'm outta here, Chief," Grant said. "Have all the friends and relatives mustered around 2125 hours."

"Roger that, sir!"

On his way to the torpedo room to start getting ready and pick up his gear, he made a detour and stopped by the Captain's stateroom. The steel door was ajar, the curtain pushed aside. "Sir?"

Stafford was sitting at his desk sorting through his mail. He peered over the top of his wire-rimmed bifocals. "Come on in, Grant." He put the two page letter on the desk, a small photo attached to the corner. "Just reading my niece Patty's letter. She had to tell her uncle about the money the tooth fairy left her."

Grant leaned toward the desk, looking at a toothless, smiling face in the photo. The little girl was wearing a *Bluefin* baseball cap, the printing on the paper indicative of a six year old. "Uh, she's very cute, sir. Must be hard for her to whistle, though."

Stafford laughed and nodded in agreement. "Yeah. Her three brothers give her a hard time."

"Sir, it's about time for me to head out. My ride's on the way," he grinned as he pointed overhead.

Stafford took a final sip of black coffee as he stood up. "Guess that's my cue to man the Conn. Anything else we can do for you?"

"No, sir, just keep the *Bluefin* trim and aim me in the right direction."

Stafford acknowledged with a quick smile, knowing the orders Commander Stevens had and what he was preparing to do.

Ten minutes later, Grant was outfitted in his thermal underwear, with the rest of his diving gear spread out around him in precise order. There was a tapping on the watertight door and he responded, "Come."

Master Chief Davis walked in, carrying a cup of coffee. "Hope I didn't keep ya waiting, sir. There was a slight disagreement between a couple of the boys in Sonar."

"No problem, Master Chief."

"Sir, can I have one of my men get ya something to drink?"

"No thanks." He reached down and picked up his bulky drysuit, a special suit used for diving in frigid water. "But I could use your help with this."

Except for the arms, leg cuffs and the area that fit around the face, the butyl rubber was covered with canvas to prevent tearing of the rubber itself. Davis held the suit while Grant stepped in through the opening in back, an opening from just below the neck to the butt. As if it were a pull-over sweater, he put his head through the neck opening, pushed his arms down the sleeves, then adjusted the rubber around his face. Chief Davis twisted the excess section of rubber in the back forming a knot, sealing the suit. Then he put the knife and web belt around Grant, double-checked the seal on the chest canister and gave Grant a thumb's up.

Davis carried one of the cocoons as Grant followed behind with his swim fins, mask and the second cocoon. He walked through the narrow passageway, then followed Davis and climbed the ladder to the 01 level, catching curious stares from the submariners, especially after seeing the unusual breathing apparatus on his chest.

"Hold it a minute, Master Chief." He walked toward the ladder leading up to the Conn and called: "Captain?"

Stafford leaned over the rail, looking down through the opening. "Well, Commander, from the looks of your outfit, I guess this is where you want to get off."

Grant smiled. "Yes, sir."

"Let us know if we can be of further assistance with those orders of yours."

"I'll keep that in mind, Captain. And thanks for the ride!"

Captain Reggie Stafford snapped a smart salute. "Good luck, sailor!"

Grant returned the salute, then turned and followed the COB to the escape chamber. They put the cocoons next to the chamber door, then Davis assisted him while he adjusted the breathing apparatus, the Draegar-rig. The old Emerson-rig and the Draegar were bubbleless and had their limited depths of 30 feet due to pure oxygen becoming toxic below that depth. Both had the reputation for leaking. When the filter granules of barylyme meet with sea water, the combination creates a caustic gas that burns the lungs and has been known to cause death. But he knew the Draeger; he'd used it hundreds of times. His experience and confidence in the rig showed as his fingers quickly went from place to place, ensuring its integrity.

He climbed the ladder leading through the inner hatch and up into the escape trunk. Not only used by divers and Special Ops teams, the escape trunk was used to exit the sub in an emergency. If it was at a depth beyond the normal range for a safe exit, the Navy would send the DSRV (Deep Submergence Rescue Vehicle), attaching it to the outer hatch.

Grant reached down as Davis handed him one cocoon at a time, then he shook the Chief's hand.

"Thanks for your help, Master Chief."

"My pleasure, sir. Come back and see us some time!" Grant grinned broadly and gave Davis a thumb's up, as COB snapped a salute. "Good luck, sir!"

Grant lowered the watertight hatch, then turned the hatch wheel, sealing it tightly. He held the mask against his face, tightened the straps on both sides, checked for air leaks, and bit down on the mouthpiece.

Below in the chamber, Davis adjusted the controls, keeping a tentative eye on the gauges, and within seconds, sea water began filling the escape trunk.

Icy cold water seeped into Grant's drysuit around his chin, sending shivers through his body as the water flowed across his throat and onto his chest. When the gauge indicated the pressure in the escape tank had equalized, he reached overhead and grabbed the hatch wheel with both hands, rotated it to the left several times, then forced it open. Immediately, he snapped a line to the cocoons, then kicked his way upward into the silence and darkness of the North Pacific.

Once outside, he pulled up the cocoons and attached one to each side of his accessory belt, then he resealed the hatch. He struck the hatch twice with the handle of his K-bar, the dull, metallic clanking sound signaling he was clear. He glanced at his illuminated wrist compass, and with one strong kick, Navy SEAL Grant Stevens shoved off from the deck, his powerful legs propelling him toward his rendezvous.

At the end of flight ops the carrier no longer needed its 30 knot speed, no longer needed the tremendous rush of wind blowing across her deck for launching and receiving her aircraft. For the past 50 minutes she'd been cruising at eight knots, a leisurely pace.

Twenty feet below the choppy sea Grant kicked his legs hard, every muscle taut as the large, black fins drove him forward, his breathing remaining even, controlled. Although the cocoons were lightweight under water, they were still a drag on his body as he fought the current...and time.

He peered down at the black shape of the *Bluefin*, hearing the deep, unchanging tone of the sub's cavitating screws. *Nice work, Captain Stafford.* The sub had maneuvered into position ahead of the carrier's port bow, maintaining a bottom depth of 80 feet until Grant locked-out and was clear. Then, she entered into a shallow dive, leveling off at 250 feet. Out of sight now, she passed directly beneath the carrier and into the dark depths of the ocean, resuming her normal operations, practicing firing solutions on the fleet.

Within a matter of minutes, water began pulsating around him as eight boilers and four, twenty-one foot screws drove more than 81,000 tons of steel toward him. There was no mistaking the rumble, like deep, exaggerated thunder rolling across the Kansas plains. He could distinguish the blurred gray shape in the darkness now, with the bow of the massive carrier no more than sixty yards in front of him. Surfacing, he looked up in awe because no matter how many times he had seen what he was now seeing, from his angle, it was still a real eye-opener.

Bobbing around in the cold, choppy water, he worked quickly and unfastened the weight belt, letting it drop from his body. He tied each cocoon to a fifty foot tether line fastened to his utility belt, then he reached for the two metal paddles attached to the plate hanging down from his backpack. The backpack was a self-contained battery that sent an electromagnetic charge through the rods to the paddles when he squeezed the trigger.

The ship was getting dangerously close, but Grant waited patiently until it was directly in front, unnecessarily reminding himself to 'not miss the boat.' He had every reason to heed his own warning. One slip would prove disastrous because the only place to go would be an involuntary passage under tons of moving steel.

With a strong kick, he stretched as far as he could, slamming each paddle against the forward port hull. The devices came into contact with the ship at the waterline and directly below the thirty ton anchor. With all his strength, he held on as the ship continued on. Even an eight knot speed put tremendous pressure on him, forcing his body backward, trying to rip his grasp from the devices.

He released the magnetic field from the right paddle, then arched his body back and with a swift motion, slammed the paddle higher against the ship. He moved higher and higher, continuously alternating paddles, as he crabbed his way out of the water. Up the side he climbed, hand over hand, as the line holding the cocoons slowly unraveled from his belt. He quickly suspended himself with a tether between the handles before snagging the line to his telescopic grapnel hook attached to his web belt. He extended the telescopic rod and reached up, catching the bottom fluke of the ship's anchor with the grapnel hook. Taking a firm grip on the pole, he released the magnets. He reattached the two electromagnets to the anchor and resnapped the tether, taking a short breather.

Readjusting his position, Grant peered up through the hawse pipe and past the shank of the anchor. The hawse pipe was the round opening where each 360 pound chain link passed through, with the anchor hanging from the last link by its shackle. *Time to move, Stevens.*

Dressed in a blue jogging suit with thermal underwear underneath, Chief Adler had just completed his second lap around the deck, keeping a wary eye out for any unexpected guests. He stopped near the hawse pipe on the port side. "Shit! He's late," Adler worried. "Christ! That water must be freezing!" he whispered through gritted teeth. His own experiences made him appreciate what 'Panther' was feeling now. Insulated suit or not, any extended period of time in cold water eventually could be hazardous, mentally and physically.

He leaned farther over the edge but couldn't

see beyond the anchor hawse, with the bow of the ship curving inward. "Shit!" He started to turn when he saw the grapnel come through the hawse, and he heard a hoarse whisper.

"Permission to come aboard, Chief!"

Adler quickly snatched the grapnel. "Gotcha, Commander!" He hooked the grapnel on the deck padeye, then gave the ready. "Go!"

Grant hauled himself up through the hawse pipe, climbed through the opening and scrambled onto the deck. They were grateful for the heavy cloud coverage and the blackness of this night. Both were the true allies in this type of operation.

Not wasting any time, Grant untied the tether line and Adler hauled up the cocoons. Sitting on the deck, Grant pulled off his swim fins and mask, stripped off his drysuit, then his thermal underwear, revealing a blue jogging suit. Bright yellow letters "USN" were embossed across the chest.

They both hustled to cram all the diving gear inside the one cocoon, then both cocoons were lowered into the chain "locker", capable of storing 1,080 feet of anchor chain. It was unlikely that anyone would notice the cocoons. His gear would be safe for now.

He tied his sneakers and pulled the jogging suit's hood close around his face, hoping to conceal some of the impressions left by the face mask and rubber suit. "Well, Chief, you ready for another lap?" he grinned.

"Let's go, sir!"

They jogged in unison down the port side of

the carrier and around the Intruders sitting in formation on the angle deck. Adler called out, "Don't know about you, sir, but I've had enough fun for one evening!"

"Let's hit the locker, Chief!"

They detoured toward the superstructure on the starboard side, through the watertight door and down to the hangar bay. Little attention was paid to them as they walked nonchalantly through the hangar bay, discussing their "improved lap times around the deck", their faces reddened from exposure to the harsh wind topside.

Finally, in the security of the EOD locker, the men shook hands, their grips firm, words sincere.

"It's really good to see you, Joe!"

"You, too, sir!"

"I guess congratulations are in order," Grant said as he pointed to the star above the chief's insignia on Adler's cap. "Can't think of anyone more deserving to be Senior Chief, Joe."

"Thanks, sir. Your evaluation helped get me that star!"

"Play your cards right on this one and you'll probably have another one to sport around!" Adler just smiled and nodded.

Grant stripped off his damp jogging suit and glanced around the locker as Adler tossed him a towel. All the diving gear and 'tools of the trade' of the Explosive Ordnance Disposal team were methodically arranged and stored within the compact room, ready on a moment's notice. Small bins with spare parts, assorted safeing pins for the ship's ordnance, and various tools lined the after bulkhead. A row of steel trunks, stacked high, was against the side of the locker. The communications gear was arranged on the desk: radio, headsets, earphones, satellite uplink transmitter, and walkie-talkies placed in their chargers, everything he'd need.

"Any 'poop' from Washington yet?" Grant asked as he rubbed the towel across his chest.

"Not since this morning. The NIS officer, Commander Simmons, dropped me a note when I was topside. Said he'd like to get up to speed on this thing when you're ready. You can use the phone on the bulkhead next to the bunk, extension 1084. When you're ready to contact Morelli, the satcom's in the desk drawer, sir." Grant nodded as he changed into a fresh jogging suit then picked up the earphones. Adler said, "I'll have one of my men retrieve your gear from the chain locker before dawn, sir. He can shove it into one of our equipment bags. Nobody'll be the wiser."

"Very well."

"Unless you need anything else, sir, I'll go turn in. You take my bunk here. And you don't have to worry about being bothered by the rest of the team tonight."

"You go 'head. I'll make my call then hit the sack myself. And thanks, Joe."

"For what?" Adler grinned, as he stepped outside the vault-like door.

Grant familiarized himself with the equipment and his new surroundings. It was midnight when he placed the call. He stood in front of the bunks, scrutinizing the room, until he heard a relieved voice: "Are you there, Grant?"

"Yes, sir. We're ready here, Admiral. I'll report to you every twelve hours, sir, unless there's an emergency."

"Understood. And I'll contact Kodiak and the other three sites, correct?" Morelli had been through the battles of Korea and Vietnam. Even so, he reached for a bottle of Rolaids.

"Yes, sir. We don't want anyone to be surprised. Appreciate it if you'd tell them to be on standby and to expect a call at anytime from me or the agent aboard the *Bronson*, sir."

"Very well, Commander. And speaking about that agent, are you going to be okay with him, considering your reaction to Agent Phillips?"

"Not a problem, sir. Did some checking...he's ex-Navy, a frogman. Can't be all bad."

"I should have known!" Morelli laughed.

"Oh, sir?"

"Yes, Commander?"

"Thought you'd like to know that Captain Stafford did an excellent job in getting me here, sir."

"Never a doubt. Good luck, Grant."

"Thanks, Admiral."

USS *Bronson*

Tony Mullins stepped through the bridge doorway, taking a bite from a slice of nearly burnt, buttered toast, and washed it down with a swig of strong black coffee. He would walk around the inside perimeter of the bridge one more time before he turned in, eyeing all the instruments, still amazed at the *Bronson*'s technology. As usual, all gauges were working properly. The ship's heading was SSW. The last things to check were the cameras. It was the same routine, day after day, but for him, the assignment was perfect. Maybe it still wasn't the seclusion of the Rocky Mountains, it wasn't his dream log cabin, but after nine years with the Agency, he finally had his solitude, for all intent and purposes.

Before leaving the bridge for a final check in his steel-enclosed office below deck, he paused by the window. Somewhere in the distance were the ships from the armada, protecting the *Preston*. They should be hearing from Washington some time soon. Would they or would they not be proceeding to the Korean coast, and God only knows what else? Noticing his reflection in the glass, he commented, "Not exactly Agency material." He laughed as he stroked his beard. And his light brown hair was already touching his collar. "What the hell! Nearly 40 years old...I deserve to be Mountain Man Mullins! Well, back to 'intestine city,'" he joked. Once the steel door was secured behind him, he sat down in front of the terminal and opened his logbook just as the phone rang.

"Mullins."

"Agent Mullins, this is Grant Stevens."

Mullins' back straightened. The call had come in on a secured line. The only communication he'd had the past months had been with his office at Langley or Kodiak, and always with the same people, the same voices.

"Stevens? Am I supposed to know you? And what the hell are you doing on this line?" he shouted.

Grant laughed. "No, you don't know me...yet. But I can assure you, you soon will. I'm a Navy Commander working for NIS. I report to Admiral Morelli. And I got your number from the NIS 'yellow pages.'"

Mullins detected immediately that the call wasn't from a telephone but probably from some type of communications gear. His mouth curved into a smile. "Okay so far. Where are you, Commander?"

"The *Preston*. I came aboard a few hours ago. The EOD team is supporting me here. In fact, that's where I'm calling from...the EOD locker." Mullins picked up on the 'came aboard a few hours ago' statement. His instinct told him he was talking to a Navy SEAL.

"What can I do for you, Commander?"

Grant came right to the point. "We believe there's going to be an unfriendly attempt to take the *Bronson*."

"Are you shittin' me?" Mullins jumped from his chair, knocking the coffee cup from the table, the black liquid barely missing the keyboard. Kodiak had warned him about bringing liquids into the center.

Grant went into details about the mole and his

thoughts on the Chinese troops, adding, "The EOD Senior Chief, Joe Adler, filled me in on the trawler that's been dogging the fleet. I expect this is one time its plan is to do more than just listen."

"Let me get on the horn with Kodiak," Mullins anxiously replied. "They'll probably want to make some computer changes, or whatever the hell it is they do."

"I'm sure you'll be in agreement with this, Agent Mullins, but I don't think there should be any written notes. This one's too hot."

"I agree."

Grant nodded to himself, thinking Mullins would be easy to work with. "Admiral Morelli should be updating Kodiak and the other sites right about now; I'm sure they're expecting to hear from you. And when you talk with them, ask them to keep a wary eye and ear on that trawler; they're to report immediately anything that's out of the ordinary, I don't care how the hell minor it may seem to them. Chief Adler's going to get as much info as he can, too."

"Understood. I'll check the radar myself."

"I know you'll be available on a moment's notice, Agent Mullins," Grant smiled, realizing Mullins had no place to go anyway.

"Yeah, I'll be here. And I'll try and dig up some more information, see if we can find out who's on the *Rachinski*. Let me know how to reach you."

Grant supplied him with the information, then added, "I'll be snooping around the ship most of the time, so let's set up a contact time of, say,

0100 hours. I'll call you."

"Got it. Look, Commander, there's too much serious shit we've got to worry about. Let's drop the formality...just call me Tony."

"Well, hell, Tony, why don't you just call me 'Commander'?" He immediately laughed then added, "Just kidding. 'Grant's' fine." Both of them realized they were quickly developing a friendship under extraordinary circumstances. "One more thing, Tony. Make sure that special equipment is ready. And while you're at it, check your diving gear. If we're lucky, maybe you won't have to use either." The 'special equipment' was the *Bronson's* self-destruct mechanism, a last resort.

"One step ahead of you. That's part of my daily routine."

Grant nodded to himself. "Somehow, Tony, I get the impression you're not typical Agency, if you get my drift. And believe me...that was meant as a compliment!"

Mullins laughed and tugged on his beard. "Ya know, it wasn't too long ago I told myself exactly that!"

"Listen, Tony, hope you understand why we didn't bring you in on this sooner."

"Sure…not a problem. It's all to do with 'keeping things close to the vest', right?"

"Roger that!"

Grant pulled off the sweatsuit and dropped it at the foot of the bunk. He stepped into the freshwater shower to rinse off the saltwater, lingering there briefly. The warm water beat on his shoulders and back as he rested his forehead and palm against the smooth stainless steel.

Grabbing the towel from a hook, he dried off, punched the pillow into a contorted shape, then stretched his body out on top of the blanket. Arms folded behind his head, he stared into the darkness. Every job he'd been involved with in Vietnam, South and Central America, or Libya, whether SEALs or Intel, it was the excitement, the prospect of confrontation. The game was always the same: the mission came first, the survival of his team members second, and finally, his own survival...and screw the bastards on the other side. Surprise them, kill everything when ordered to, let God sort them out, and disappear as fast as you struck. No explanation sounded completely reasonable, but he admitted there were times he questioned his motivation. His ability was never in question, never in doubt...the way it was supposed to be. The question was why? Why did he do it? The generic answer of preserve and defend somehow didn't fit in this game. He reasoned that his way was just another way to get it done. He turned over and closed his eyes. This wasn't the time to question. There rarely was such a time.

Kodiak - Tuesday, January 28 - 0100 hours

"Christ!" Jeff Holland slammed the receiver down into its cradle. "Get an alert out. I want everyone back here in ten minutes! And that includes the Marines!"

"Yes, sir!" Ensign Tim Baker ran to the console, sending the signal. "Done, sir," he called from the opposite side of the room. Even without smiling, the dimples in Baker's cheeks stood out as plain as day.

Holland swung his chair around. Sitting at the next console, staring in bewilderment at Holland, was Lieutenant Pat Townsend. He and Lieutenant(j.g.) Frank Stillman, Weapons Officers, controlled the surface radar, weapons, and the threat board. Townsend leaned forward and immediately started cracking his knuckles. "What? What the hell's goin' on?" he asked, his brown eyes searching Holland's face, waiting for an answer.

"That was Admiral Morelli at NIS." Holland pushed the chair back, balancing it on the two back legs. "All this shit that's happening with China and Russia? They're pretty sure it's the *Bronson* the Commies are really after."

Townsend's jaw dropped. "You're shittin'!"

"I wouldn't shit you, Pat. He didn't give me all the details, but I'd have to suspect an NIS officer's aboard the *Preston*. I guess he's a 'spook' trying to uncover a mole."

Townsend's voice went an octave lower, turning into a harsh whisper. "Mole? A fuckin' mole? Oh, man, the shit's gonna fly now. Where? Where is he?"

"Morelli didn't say specifically, but he--"

"Sir, excuse me," interrupted Ensign Baker,

"but it's Agent Mullins, on the *Bronson*." He handed the phone to Holland.

"Holland."

"Commander, you talk to Admiral Morelli yet?"

"Just did. Christ! What's going on?"

"Don't know much more than you," replied Mullins. "I've been in contact with Grant Stevens--Commander Grant Stevens. He's the NIS guy on the carrier reporting to Morelli." Holland was shaking his head, acknowledging the information, still staring at Townsend. "By the way, as a side note," continued Mullins, "I'm pretty certain he's a Navy SEAL."

For several more minutes they spoke, Mullins revealing as much as he knew. Holland stood slack-jawed, keeping his stare fixed on Townsend.

There were eight random light flashes on the keypad by the steel entry door. The Marine guard looked up at the television monitor, the images showing in sharp black and white. He entered the response code into his keypad, and the heavy door slowly swung inward, only one third the way open before the rest of the officers and Marines rushed in. Some of them hadn't been off duty very long, their sleep interrupted, their clothes disheveled. Beneath their bulky parkas, hanging off their shoulders, were Uzi submachine guns.

Bob Little, the second senior officer at the center, was pulling off his thick gloves and parka. The temperature was 30 degrees below zero in Kodiak that day. "What the hell's going on--?" he asked as he smoothed back his black hair.

Holland held up his hand, silencing Little. "Okay, Agent Mullins, I'll wait for your call." He handed the receiver to Ensign Baker, as he shook his head. He stared up through clear gray eyes at each of the men surrounding him. "Gentlemen, we've got us a crisis."

After he explained, the first obvious question was asked by Frank Stillman. "Sir, aren't we even going to use the "Zippo?" Stillman referenced the nickname they had given the special weapon aboard the *Bronson*.

Holland shook his head. "Our orders from the beginning have been to wait, wait until there was imminent danger to South Korea. If we used "Zippo" now, it'd appear that we were the aggressor, you know, Geneva Convention and world opinion shit. We know what it can do, but we don't have just cause...not yet. Besides, it's out of our hands right now." He paused, picking a red thread from his beige corduroy slacks. "Admiral Morelli's going to hold off trying to get a SEAL team aboard the *Bronson*. Even though they've probably got ways to get aboard without detection, with that fucking trawler so close, he doesn't want to risk tipping the Russians off. He's relying on some commander to find out who the mole is...and find him before we have to go with a contingency plan."

Bob Little agreed and added, "Look, we don't know how or even when they're planning to hit the *Bronson*. We've got no choice but to wait. All the intel suggests she's the target, and that's all we know." He rolled the tip of his pencil-thin, black mustache between his fingertips. "But there's a lot we can do in the meantime to protect Uncle Sam's investment." He looked at Holland. "We'll talk with the other sites." Holland nodded, then reached for the phone. "Double up at your stations," Little ordered. "I want all heads working this."

He walked to the rear of the center, where Lieutenant Michael Antonelli and Lieutenant(j.g.) Cliff Patten were already testing their systems. Both had fleet experience and were put in charge of radar guidance and navigation of the missile launches.

"We're on it, sir," smiled Antonelli without even looking up.

Little turned his attention toward the Marines. "Marines!"

Eight booming voices answered in unison: "Sir!"

"It may not just be the *Bronson* we need to worry about."

Sergeant Bruce Watson stepped forward. "I understand, sir. My men are ready, sir!"

"Very well, Sergeant." Little couldn't hide his brief smile before turning to his own young officers, Ensign Baker and Lieutenant(j.g.) Clark Young. Both were assigned as software and hardware technicians for the TSC-MK1. They had top secret (code word) clearances and had assisted Dr. Hiram Mertz, the computer's designer/ inventor, in bringing it all together.

"Lieutenant Young and Ensign Baker, each of you get a sidearm from Sergeant Watson's armory." Holland shifted his stare to Ensign Baker. "Turn on the laser security net. No one comes or goes without positive visual ID, understood?"

"Aye, aye, sir!"

CHAPTER FIVE

USS *Preston* - January 28 - 0530 hours

A full clip rested on the corner of the desk, with two extras in the cocoon, ready to be loaded into the .45. Grant wiped down the heavy revolver known for its "immediate stopping power", guaranteed to fell an assailant. The life-saving weapon had been with him in Vietnam and Libya, becoming another component of his life. The clip locked in place as he rammed it up into the handle and jacked the slide to the rear, putting a round in the chamber. He glanced down at the cocoon, then reached in and pulled out the submachine gun, laying it across his lap. Although compact, the Uzi was capable of firing up to 500 rounds per minute. Methodically, the weapon was disassembled then reassembled, a procedure he'd done literally with his eyes closed, preparing for the times he'd be operating in the blackness of night. Both weapons, along with ten, fifty round clips of ammo were placed back into the cocoon, ready when, and if, he'd need them.

He put on his khaki trousers and shirt, then slipped the nylon web belt through the loops, feeding the end through the glistening brass buckle, when he heard the door unlock.

"Mornin'," Adler said, handing Grant a cup of steaming, black coffee.

"Mornin', Joe. Thanks." Grant smiled broadly, reaching for the hot cup. "Well, what do you think?"

He stood tall in his "new" uniform, the work khakis with the insignia of an E-7, CPO (Chief Petty Officer). All of this--the uniform, the EOD locker, the carrier itself--would allow him to blend right in, giving him the freedom he needed to carry out his undercover assignment.

Adler laughed, creases forming around his blue eyes. "Well, sir, this may be the one and only time I'll outrank you!"

Grant slapped his friend on the back. "Hell, Joe, you always did. No officer worth his salt could possibly survive this 'canoe club' without a top notch CPO--pure fact! Besides, with all the shit I've put you through, now's your chance to take it out on me!"

Adler shook his head, dead serious. "No way, sir. It'll never happen."

January 28 - 0900 hours

CPO Stevens was seen rushing down passageways, more than likely on his way to "put out another fire." He was blending in just as he thought he might. What seemed like innocent conversations and questions, handled expertly, could prove to be extremely helpful in his quest. But trying to cover eleven decks worth of carrier and trying to intercept messages, seemed a formidable task. Chief Adler and the rest of the EOD team could only offer a limited amount of assistance, having to maintain their normal routine. But if and when the situation heated up, Adler had permission to assist Grant full time.

During flight ops, the EOD team members had no choice but to be at their stations on the flight deck or hangar bay where the aircraft weapons were loaded and unloaded. But for Grant, flight ops might prove to be his opportunity. All the ships in the task force would be active during flight ops. It would be the best time for the mole to make a move, make contact, more than likely at night. He knew there'd be communication between the mole and the *Rachinski*. Tonight 'Chief' Stevens would lock himself in the EOD locker, monitoring the airwaves. But luck was still going to play an important role.

Bridge, USS *Preston*

Captain Donovan swung his chair around, bellowing a new order. "Officer of the Deck, bring her into the wind. Prepare to launch aircraft."

"Aye, aye, Captain. Helmsman, right 15 degrees rudder; set new course zero four five degrees."

"Aye, aye, sir. Coming right...at zero three zero degrees...at zero four zero degrees...steady on zero four five degrees, sir."

"Lee-helm, make turns for 30 knots," ordered

OOD Crawley.

"Thirty knots. Aye, aye, sir," responded Petty Officer Hayes. Standing at the lee-helm station, he grabbed both handles, the left controlling engine speed, and the right, the rudder. He cranked both handles all the way forward, then down. The two indicator handles stopped at the "Full Speed" position. He watched the dial face of the lee-helm, until the Engine Room swung its arrow forward to match the position of the handles. "Lee-helm answers turns for 30 knots, sir."

"Very well," replied Crawley. "Captain, we're at zero four five degrees, making turns for 30 knots; estimate three minutes to full speed, sir."

At three minutes, the helmsman called out, "Sir, we're at 30 knots."

"Air Boss, launch aircraft," ordered Captain Donovan.

January 28 - 1955 hours

Grant sat in the mess hall and downed the last mouthful of cold milk then rolled the empty glass between his palms. He watched everyone, looking for any kind of sign, relying on his instincts, his thoughts in constant motion. He pushed the cuff of his sleeve back and glanced at his watch. It was time to make a quick run to the locker.

Once sealed behind the steel door of the EOD locker, he dropped his cap on the bed, then slipped the headset on. Munching on a Snickers bar, he started adjusting the radio dial, when every muscle froze with the sound of two Russian voices conversing in their native language. "There you are, you sonofabitch!" he mumbled as he scribbled the radio frequency on the calendar.

One Russian asked, "When will it be ready?"

"Tomorrow night."

"That's very good news."

Grant was pacing now. He pressed the headset against his ear. "Come on, come on, tell me what I need to hear."

"We will talk again, Comrade," said the voice on the *Rachinski*. There was a click...end of transmission.

Grant threw the headset on the desk, cracked open the hatch making sure no one was close by, then stepped outside, ready to make a dash across the hangar bay. The roar of jet engines told him flight ops were underway. "Shit! Where the hell am I gonna go?" There were thousands of places for someone to hide, and he wasn't even sure the Russian was on the carrier.

He went back inside the locker, with the Russian's words running through his mind, making him wonder what was 'going to be ready tomorrow.' He stood in front of the desk, staring at the communications equipment. Even though the transmission had some interference, there was something familiar about one of the voices. He grabbed the headset.

"Tony!"

Mullins swallowed a mouthful of Coke. "Yeah. I tried to reach you earlier; guess you were out snoopin'."

"Did you get anything on the trawler?"

"Yeah. That's what I've been waiting to tell you. Found out there's a KGB boy on board by the name of 'Vernichenko.'"

"Christ! That's it! That's the voice."

"What voice?"

"As luck would have it, I intercepted their conversation just a while ago."

"No shit?"

"No shit. Sergei Vernichenko, right?"

"Yeah. Right. Say...you wanna tell me how you know a KGB officer?"

"Come on, Agent Mullins. You mean I really gotta tell you something you probably already know?" Mullins laughed. Just as Grant believed, Mullins did his own checking. "Listen, Tony, I need you to call Kodiak and tell them not to interfere with any of the trawler's transmissions. Vernichenko said something would be ready tomorrow night."

"What? What's gonna be ready?"

"That's what I need to confirm. I'll wait here ten minutes for you to contact me."

"Later," replied Mullins.

January 28 - 2005 hours

New to the ship, Seaman Barry Koosman was coming off watch and simply took a wrong turn, down the wrong deck. He stopped in front of the Damage Control locker trying to get his bearings just as the door opened. His reactions were not as quick as Alexei Pratopapov's. Before he had time to react, a powerful hand grabbed him by his blue denim work shirt. The young seaman was spun around, a hand clasped tightly over his mouth as the other grabbed his hair, pulling his head back. In one lightning, swift motion, before any sound could escape from the mouth, it was all over, leaving no bruises, no indication of foul play. His neck snapped; his body twitched as he was dragged the rest of the way into the locker.

Alexei stretched the body out on the floor, closed the door, then screamed to himself not to panic. He stared down at the body by his feet, its head resting in an unnatural position, the eyelids still wide open in shock. "You dumb fool! Why did you have to come here now?" he muttered through clenched teeth. It was more of an angry exclamation than a question. *Things one never forgets--how to kill*.

Somewhere in the distance there were voices. He stood next to the door, pressing his palms and cheek against it, listening. Soon, the passageway was quiet again. He backed up and stumbled over Koosman's foot, falling against the locker, the noise echoing in his ears. Afraid to move, he held his breath while he listened. No one came. He made a decision...leave the body, return later. It would have to look like an accident, but he needed to think it out, come back when it was quiet.

He was almost clear of the area, when he stopped short, thinking he'd better not leave the walkie-talkie, then he ran back to the closet. He fumbled with the towel, ripped the walkie-talkie from it, finally stuffing it down the front of his shirt. He threw the face towel back inside the fan vent, then bolted from the compartment.

"Sir, you wanted to see me?" asked OOD Crawley as he entered the Sea Cabin.

Donovan looked up from his papers. "What? Oh, yes. The Admiral's requested we cancel GQ tonight."

"Cancel GQ, sir?"

Donovan glared at the OOD. "You heard me. The Admiral and I agreed that the men have been under a lot of pressure. Everyone could use a break, no matter how minor it may seem to you, Mr. Crawley."

"Yes, sir. I understand, sir."

"I'm glad you do. Now, pass the word."

"Yes, sir." Crawley had a hand on the door-knob, when Donovan called to him. "Frank, I guess we're all a little anxious and tired."

"Yes, Captain. Goodnight."

As taps sounded at 2200 hours, the interior of the ship went dark, except for the red passageway lights leading to the exterior watertight doors. At 2235 hours, a lone figure hurried down the passageway, unlocking the door to the Damage Control locker. Beads of sweat formed across his brow as he bent down to the lifeless body, dragging it through the doorway and across the deck.

He lifted the body to a limp, standing position, then released it, watching as it somersaulted over the metal ladder, hitting the deck twelve feet below with a sickening *thud*, laying in a crumpled mass. Alexei felt a mental grimace as the young seaman's head hit the steel tile-covered deck. He turned quickly, went to the end of the passageway and stopped. His training dictated that he check the area one more time. Satisfied, he turned and left.

January 29 - 0530 hours

"Any luck with that tour of the bridge, Chief?" asked Grant as he guided the razor across his chin.

Adler secured the locker door, then sat on the edge of the communication's desk. "Yeah, whenever you're ready, sir."

Grant rinsed away the last traces of shaving cream then dried his face. He brushed back strands of hair hanging over his forehead, and one glance in the mirror told him it was time for a haircut. *Who's got time?*

He leaned back against the edge of the sink, folding his arms across his chest. Adler observed the square jaw clenching tight, noticed the intensity in the brown eyes as Grant stared at him. "Joe, we don't have too much time. The conversation I heard last night confirmed that. There's something on the *Rachinski* we've got to know about...or do something about."

"How do ya know?"

Grant stuck his hands in his back pockets and walked across the room. “Part what I heard and part gut feeling."

Adler took a sip of coffee. "Let me know what I can do."

Grant nodded several times, acknowledging Adler's request while he buttoned his khaki shirt. "First, I've got to talk with Mullins, then we'll take that tour of the bridge."

Both of them snapped their heads around when they heard the tap of metal against metal. Joe went to the door, peering through the spyhole next to the door. "It's just Brockton," he said as he unlocked the door.

Petty Officer Second Class Jerry Brockton, the youngest of the EOD team, closed the door, locking it behind him. He unzipped his green EOD jacket, removed his hat and smoothed back a curl of blond hair. "Sorry, Chief, Commander, but I thought you'd want to know. I just came from the flight deck. Word is that a sailor was found dead late last night, a seaman by the name of Koosman." Grant's back stiffened immediately, and he fixed his stare on the young petty officer, a verbal question not even necessary. "I think he fell down a ladder, sir, somewhere on deck three. Busted neck. There was evidence of some spilled liquid, like Coke, at the top and they figured he slipped."

"Did they find a Coke can or paper cup?" asked Grant with a lowered voice, the sarcasm unmistakable.

"Don't know, sir," answered Brockton, shaking his head.

Grant went silent in total concentration. The two EOD men stared at him, Adler finally saying, "Thanks, Jerry. Go get your gear. I'll be on deck shortly."

"Right, Chief." Brockton shot a quick look at Grant before he left the locker.

Adler put on his jacket. "Do you think it was...?"

Grant nodded. "It's gotta be; that's too damn much of a coincidence." He picked up the head-set. "We've got a lot to do, Joe. Listen, before you go topside, can you get a message to the NIS officer? I think it's advantageous we finally make contact." Adler was half-way out the open door when Grant called: "Joe, keep your fingers crossed that we can draw that goddamn trawler close-in tonight."

Adler grinned, already having a good idea of what Grant had in mind. "Will do!"

Grant and NIS Officer Lieutenant Commander Brad Simmons each knew the other was onboard, Simmons having full details of Grant's mission. An NIS officer is assigned to a carrier for every cruise. But making contact wasn't necessary until now. Simmons would be the officer in charge of investigating the death of Seaman Koosman.

Impatiently, Grant pounded his fist on the desk. "Come on, Tony. Pick up! Pick up!"

"Mullins!"

"Christ! I thought you abandoned ship!"

"Hell, no, just a quick trip to take a leak. What's up?"

"They found some kid dead early this morning."

"Oh, shit. What happened?"

Tony listened. His question was more like a statement. "You don't think it was an accident, do you?"

"I think that kid was in the wrong place at the wrong time."

Mullins scratched his beard. "What's next?"

"Call Kodiak. Ask them to maneuver the *Bronson* closer to the carrier. We have to 'reel in' that trawler. Try to get it less than a mile from the carrier."

"Do you want me to confirm with you after I talk with Kodiak?"

"Can't. I've got some investigative work to do. I'll call you at 1100 hours."

"What happens after I'm in range?"

"Adler and I are gonna use the MSV." The Motorized Submersible Vehicle weighed six pounds, was approximately 3-1/2 feet in length with the diameter of a saucer, capable of traveling as far as two miles on its small battery charge, at a depth of ten feet. Encased within its nose was a miniature camera and a trailing antenna that allowed the pictures to be sent by a transistorized transmitter up to a distance of 15 miles. As soon as it started submerging, sea water energized a special chemical battery activating its motor and a ten-foot length of antenna slowly unraveled.

"Good move!" Mullins remarked. "What time-frame are we talking here?"

Grant looked at his watch. "Have them shoot for 1830, starboard side, at about our zero two zero degrees. That'll be a good point for us and should give us enough time, as long as the trawler takes the bait. You stay on the horn with Kodiak till you're in place tonight. Then call me. We've got to start moving, Tony."

"I hear ya."

January 29 - 0700 hours

Fresh aromas of bacon and eggs lingered in the mess hall, but 'CPO' Stevens and Lieutenant Commander Simmons were seen only having a morning cup of coffee. The enlisted mess was a good place to pick up any 'scuttlebutt.'

Grant leaned on the edge of the metal table, keeping his voice low. "Have you talked to anyone, Brad?"

Simmons poured some cream in the coffee, stirring it continuously as he nodded. "Interviewed Doc Matthews and two pilots, a Lieutenant Hawthorne and Lieutenant Allen." He licked the spoon then dropped it on the stainless steel table. "Hawthorne and Allen found the kid."

"Anything specific about the body?"

"You mean, other than a broken neck and a gash in the back of his head?" he said with a twisted smile.

Grant held up his hand, as if conceding. "Okay, okay. You know what I mean."

Simmons stared into his cup, then looked up at Grant. "Nothing else. The gash on his head probably happened when he hit the step. There was a smear of blood on one of the top steps."

Several sailors with trays of food passed by their table, eyeing them warily. The officers waited patiently until the men passed. Grant swallowed a mouthful of coffee then asked, "Can you show me where it happened then take me to see the body in sickbay?"

"Sure," replied Simmons, as both of them stood. "Looking for anything special?"

"Yeah. As a matter of fact, I am."

Bridge - USS *Preston* - 0945 hours

"Morning, CAG."

"Hey! Chief Adler. What brings EOD to the Roost? Have ya lost a bomb? Should we be evacuating the area?"

Adler laughed. "No, sir. I promised Chief Stevens here a tour of the bridge and Roost, since this is his first cruise on the *Preston*. Is that okay, sir?"

CAG reached out for Grant's hand, gripping it firmly. "Sure; no problem. Welcome aboard, Chief."

"Thanks," smiled Grant, "it's good to be here, sir."

"Sorry it's not a more enjoyable cruise, Chief, what with China and all."

Grant nodded. "I hear ya, CAG."

For the next fifteen minutes Grant and Adler walked the bridge, Grant listening, observing, occasionally asking a seemingly innocent question. He lingered briefly by the quartermaster's table where the logbook was kept. His mind 'photographed' the two pages used to record the time of day when the captain, OOD, quartermaster, and others came and went from the bridge.

The Air Boss picked up the phone, then called to CAG, "Tomcats are on their final approach."

Both Dodson and Morehouse raised binoculars. Dodson returned to the Roost and recorded on the glass the positions of the F-14s. "Jesus. This weather's a bitch," he mumbled looking at the threatening gray mass of clouds on the horizon.

"CAG," Adler said, "I'm going to take Chief Stevens down to the flight deck while the 14's come in."

Morehouse turned. "Sorry I couldn't give you the grand tour, Chief." He motioned over his shoulder with his thumb, indicating the arriving planes.

"No problem, sir," replied Grant.

Morehouse hustled back to the Roost and answered the phone. "Oh, shit. Willy's comin' in first." CAG searched the darkened sky with binoculars and called, "Hey, Chief Adler! Don't forget to tell Chief Stevens about Willy!"

Normally, ships that make up a task force receive their orders from the carrier over the task group radio frequencies. Ships would not arbitrarily change course without the carrier's permission and knowledge, unless the ship received a 'flash' message from a higher authority. For the *Bronson*, those orders would come from Vice Admiral Morelli, who wore the 'hat' of Chief of Naval Investigative Service. Protocol dictated he pass them through the Fleet Admiral stationed in Hawaii, CINCPACFLEET (Commander in Chief Pacific Fleet).

At 1815 hours, Jeff Holland in Kodiak radioed the *Preston* via satellite uplink. "*Preston*, this is the *Bronson*. Over."

"Go ahead, *Bronson*. Over."

"I am in receipt of flash message through CINCPACFLEET. At this time, I have been advised to change course and proceed independently. Will advise. *Bronson* out."

With orders to "proceed independently", the *Bronson* would no longer have to receive permission from the carrier to change course. Responding to commands from Kodiak, the *Bronson* came to course three three zero, adjusted its speed to 15 knots and headed in the direction of the *Preston*.

On the forward deck of the destroyer stood Tony Mullins, night vision binoculars hung around his neck, the fur collar of his leather flight jacket pulled up to his ears. Just the opposite of CAG's concern, Mullins worried that the current weather conditions would clear sooner than forecasted, as an occasional glimpse of the moon broke through the cloud coverage. "Bad timing. Don't need any bright sky tonight." He turned the brim of his New

York Yankees' baseball cap to the back, raised the binoculars and scanned the surrounding area. "Where the hell are you, Mr. Russkie?"

The *Bronson* reduced speed to eight knots as it approached the *Preston* at 1,200 yards from starboard aft, cruising along until it was parallel with the carrier. Kodiak adjusted the speed, gradually bringing the *Bronson* to a zero two zero degrees position as Grant had requested, then held her there. Her wake began to act like a fishing line, reeling it farther out, waiting for a big "fish" to take the bait.

Mullins walked aft for a clearer view. "Yes!" he shouted. The *Rachinski* was following the destroyer, about 1,000 yards behind it, steadily pulling closer to the starboard bow of the carrier. That's when the *Bronson* held her speed, keeping the *Rachinski* at the designated position.

Mullins reached for the walkie-talkie hanging on his belt and put in the call.

"Adler here."

Mullins responded, "Chief, the 'fish' is hooked!"

Adler grinned. "Understood. Stay with me, sir."

Thirty feet above the waterline, Grant and Joe positioned themselves inside one of the outcroppings. Outcroppings were located on the port and starboard sides of the bow, protruding out and slightly below the flight deck. They were used to store life vests and canisters containing life rafts. Each canister rested at the top of two rails. If there was a need to abandon ship, the life vests would be thrown over the side to the men in the water, while the canisters were shoved down the rails, falling to the ocean. Normally, only a few were supposed to have a key to access this area through the scuttle, but NIS was able to provide a master key for Grant, along with anything else he requested. "It's amazing what you can get with who you know," he had laughed when Morelli handed him the envelope containing the key.

Grant was on his stomach as he lowered the MSV down to the water, while Adler handled the walkie-talkie, with minimal conversation passing between him and Mullins. Grant guided the MSV by remote control on an intercept course toward its destination--the *Rachinski*. He kept the speed at six knots, just under its eight knot limit, trying to conserve the battery power. They spoke just above a whisper. "There it is, Joe. Now, if I can just...maneuver it..." Only ten feet below the surface, the MSV was subject to the undulation of the ocean. Grant kept his hand in constant motion with the control, gingerly maneuvering the vehicle nearer to the bow of the trawler. "Bingo!"

Adler leaned closer to the nine inch monitor, propped up on the deck in front of Grant. "What? What's that? Holy shit! Is that a mini-sub?"

"Yeah," Grant replied matter-of-factly, "it's a goddamn mini-sub." He shot a quick glance at Adler. "Relay this info to Tony, then tell him to send a 'well done' to Kodiak." He looked away from Adler's stare.

This Russkie had disguised herself well. She

wasn't a typical trawler. Installed beneath her hull, at midships, was a matte black, stainless steel capsule, specifically designed to resemble a torpedo tube. The inside of the capsule was fashioned to hold a two-man mini-sub. Once it was in place, it would only need the sea water to rush in, enabling it to complete the mission it was designed for.

Adler passed on the message then switched off the walkie-talkie, putting it on the deck. "You knew! How the fuck did you know...sir?"

Grant started bringing in the MSV, staring out across the darkened water, then looked down at the screen. "Sergei Vernichenko, the KGB officer on the *Rachinski*."

Adler still looked puzzled. "Yeah? So?"

"In '62 I was on one of my first jobs, let's just say, in a southern region. Vernichenko was a Russian Naval officer, a submarine officer assigned there. They were finalizing their experiments with--"

"With mini-subs," Adler interrupted. His eyes widened as he realized what Grant was talking about. "Not during the missile crisis?" he asked in astonishment. "You were there?"

Grant's face was expressionless, then he looked away, continuing to haul the MSV up the side of the carrier. Adler knew he wouldn't get any further explanation, at least not now. Grant focused his eyes on the MSV, but his mind wandered back in time, back to Cuba.

A U-2 spy plane had photographed a SAM missile site about eight miles away from what looked like an old tobacco barn. A sharp-eyed seaman, stationed in the Photo Reconnaissance Center in Virginia, noticed cars parked around the building, immediately bringing it to the attention of his CO.

Grant and his team were sent in to set up miniature transceivers, strategically placing them in the loft and around the outside of the tobacco barn. Prepared for any situation, each SEAL carried with him pencil flares, an Uzi and three extra clips that held fifty rounds each, a .45 with two extra clips of seven rounds each, medical kit with atropine, thermite grenades, two high explosive (HE) hand grenades, and a flashlight.

They listened and waited, remaining hidden for two days. Burrowing themselves beneath the tobacco stalks and leaves, completely camouflaged, their suspicions were finally confirmed. Their orders stated that when they were certain all the Russians were inside, they were to strike...and they did, swiftly, accurately, precisely. Within minutes, their mission was over--the building, experimental subs, the Russians--all destroyed, except for one. That one Grant Stevens would not forget. There had been a brief glimpse of a face in a vehicle, a face unable to hide its rage. But it had been the distinctive sound of a voice that played over and over in his brain like a broken record, the voice he heard in his headset for two days--a gravely, boastful voice--the proud, Georgian accent belonging to Sergei Vernichenko.

CHAPTER SIX

January 30 - Midnight

"Say again, Commander?"

"The Russian's right here, on the carrier, sir."

"You'd better be goddamn sure," growled Morelli, while he loosened his tie.

Grant's back straightened from a response he hadn't expected. "I am, sir.

"Good Christ!" Morelli stood abruptly, the back of his knees sending his chair against the wall. He wiped a hand across his face, then picked up the smoldering cigar from the ashtray, rolling it between his fingers.

"Everything adds up, sir--the conversations I've intercepted, reports I've seen. Simmons and I have been working closely, comparing notes. That seaman's death confirmed everything. The kid was murdered, Admiral."

Morelli knew there were times he aggravated the shit out of Grant, and this was one of them. "How in the hell did you reach that conclusion?"

Grant began to stiffen against the questions, but he maintained his composure. "It was made to look as though he slipped on some spilled Coke, but Doc Matthews said the kid didn't have any Coke in his stomach, there wasn't any around the body, and only a small amount on the upper deck."

Morelli sat back down, put his foot on the desk and pushed himself deeper into his leather chair, all the while gnawing on the Havana. "Maybe he was clumsy and just tripped."

Grant frowned, but held his tongue. "Brad and I talked with Doc Matthews. He said for the size of the gash in the back of Koosman's head, there was only a minuscule amount of blood. If he was only unconscious when he went down, there should have been a pool of blood under him. Besides, Admiral, that's why they wear rubber soled shoes, so they don't slip...uh, you already know that, sir." A 'black shoe' himself, Morelli had come up through the ranks to earn his third gold admiral's star.

"You're right, and I'm still listening."

"Our conclusion came from the way the body was found, sir. Again, no blood."

"And what does that prove?"

"Well, sir, Doc let us see the body in sickbay. He pointed out some blood that had pooled just under the skin, behind his neck and shoulders, which means he had to be on his back right after he died for that to happen. He said rigor mortis had already set in. Admiral, that kid was dead for a while before he ended up at the bottom of that ladder, sir." Grant waited for a response...none came. "Brad and I searched the compartment area above the deck where the body was found, but didn't have any luck. Shit! I couldn't believe I found the towel where I did...sir."

"Towel?"

"Yes, sir. The Chief and I were in the starboard outcropping where we used the MSV. We made a final inspection before we left the area. I decided to check out the port outcropping, too, since it was a good hiding place, just like it was for us. Something caught my eye. A towel was pushed up against the back side of the fan vent. We went inside the DC locker and unscrewed the louver cover. The broken tip of an antenna was stuck in one of the loops of the towel. Our Russian friend must have been in one helluva hurry."

"Sonofabitch!"

"Yes, sir," Grant answered, relieved. "I stuffed the towel back in the vent just in case he comes back for it, or decides to use the same outcropping, but I don't think that's likely. He'll find another place."

"I guess my next question has to be, who? Do you know who the bastard is, Commander?"

"I've got it narrowed down but that's about all I can tell you now." Morelli nodded, as Grant asked, "Sir?"

Even with the seriousness of the conversation, Morelli smiled, somehow anticipating Grant Stevens was about to make a request. "Go ahead, Grant."

"Sir, is there any chance you could have orders issued for the fleet to change course, head into the Sea of Japan?"

A steady stream of cigar smoke drifted toward the ceiling. Morelli's eyes narrowed. "That's a serious request. Don't you think there's a good chance that would push the Russians and Chicoms into making a move into Korea? You've gotta give me a good reason."

Grant was shaking his head as he responded, "I still stand by my decision that they want the *Bronson*, sir. From what I could see of the mini-sub, that weapons' platform was redesigned. I'm sure that's how they plan on hauling away the SNAGS. And they're not expecting us to make the move into the Sea of Japan. They're assuming we're waiting for the Chicoms, which would then give them their chance. I think we'll catch them off guard, Admiral. And with the fleet on the move, all they'll be able to do is keep up. We can have Captain Stafford run interference by positioning the *Bluefin* between the trawler and the *Bronson*." Grant leaned back against the communication's desk, staring down at the floor. "We've gotta get our asses out of here, sir. I just need a little while longer, and this is the only way to get it."

"I'll see what I can do." He glanced at the clock above his door. "I'll call Allen Wooster, the National Security Advisor, and get back to you at 1100 hours, East Coast time."

Grant closed his eyes as he rubbed his pounding temple. Coupled with lack of sleep and the intense mental pressure, he was beginning to feel the strain. "Thanks. Oh, one more thing, sir."

Morelli had to laugh out loud this time. "Now what the hell do you want?"

"If the orders are approved, sir, can you wait till

0800 hours, my time, to pass the order on to CINCPACFLEET and issue a departure time of 0900 hours? I don't want to give the Russians any notice."

"Very well, Commander. You'll be hearing from me."

Grant took a bite from the Snicker's bar, washed it down with a swig of cold milk, then called Mullins. "Tony, listen. Contact Kodiak ASAP. Prepare them for receiving new orders."

"What the hell's happening?"

"I've asked Morelli to issue orders that will send the fleet into the Sea of Japan. It's the only way to buy more time, Tony."

Mullins detected the fatigued voice and sensed the urgency. "I know, buddy. I'll do whatever you ask, whenever. Hey, you know we're going to win this thing, don't you?"

Grant smiled. "Thanks. Go make your call."

USS *Preston* - Bridge - 0815 hours

"Edward," Captain Donovan called as he stepped through the doorway onto the bridge, motioning for the steward, who was pouring coffee for the OOD. He handed him an envelope. "See this gets into the pouch for that COD flight before it takes off." The COD was a long-range transport, but more importantly for the men aboard ship, it delivered letters to and from home.

"Certainly, Captain," Mindina responded, as he slipped the envelope into his white jacket pocket.

OOD Crawley walked over to him, a cup of steaming coffee in his hand. "Was that a letter to Koosman's folks?"

Donovan rested his chin on his fist as he leaned against the swivel chair, staring in the direction of the eastern horizon. "Haven't had to write one of those in a long time."

He glanced at his watch, abruptly turned, then motioned for Wayne Masters, the XO (Executive Officer), and Petty Officer Andrews to follow him, leading them to the Sea Cabin, one door down the passageway from the bridge. Petty Officer Andrews closed the cabin door behind them then stepped closer to the two officers. Donovan stood in the middle of the room, hands in his back pockets, glancing at the overhead with its jungle of cables and pipes. "No need to sit, gentlemen, this will be brief." He looked at Navigator Andrews, ordering, "Plot me a course to Point Juliet Alpha in the Sea of Japan and give me an eight-hour ticket. Bring it back to me ASAP and advise the quartermaster."

"Yes, sir." Andrews rushed from the cabin.

Donovan took a step, stopping in front of the porthole, hands clasped behind him, then he turned to Masters. "Wayne, we just got our orders from CINCPAC. We're to proceed into the Sea of Japan and wait for further instructions."

Masters' back stiffened, his hands balled up into tight fists next to his sides. "Has the situation heated up, sir?"

Donovan shrugged his shoulders. "The orders

just say to station ourselves off the western coast of Japan near the Island of Sado. We've got to get out of here by 0900."

"Not much notice, sir," Masters commented, glancing down at his watch.

"That's why it's time to move, XO." Donovan picked up the silver cigarette lighter from the table, flicking it on and off. "Brief the OOD and give him a leg-up on our orders...and record it in the pass-down log." As the name implied, the 'passdown log' was a continuous record of events used to keep the next watch informed.

"Yes, sir." Masters didn't need to be told the conversation was over. He left immediately.

Donovan lingered a few moments then returned to the bridge. He reached for the phone hanging from the overhead, calling Dodson. "Air Boss."

"Yes, sir?"

"Launch the E-2, then two Intruders and two Tomcats. I want them keeping the skies clear."

"Aye, aye, Captain."

As always, the Tomcats would each carry six Phoenix missiles, built specifically to defend against Russia's TU-95 Bear, feared at one time because of its deadly anti-ship missiles. But with the Phoenix, the threat was counteracted. In a simulation test, one F-14 pilot, carrying six Phoenix missiles, shot down five of six drone targets. From that moment, the Tomcat was dubbed "Fleet Defender".

Within six minutes five aircraft were catapulted

from the *Preston*'s flight deck. The task force turned northwest, sailing for the Sea of Japan, with the *Rachinski* not far behind.

Crew's Mess Hall - 0830 hours

Two sailors sat at the table, having just been relieved from watch. Jake Farley shook his egg-laden fork at Sid Neuman. "Listen, I don't care what you say, Neuman, as sure as God made silent, stinky farts...you can bet your ass something's going down."

Knowing Farley the way he did, Neuman hissed, "Yeah, right," and continued spreading strawberry jelly on his toast. He licked his fingers and stared straight into the eyes of his shipmate. "You're so full of shit, Farley."

"You mean you haven't seen that Chief, the one asking questions?" Farley said, then immediately shoved the fork into his mouth. He wiped egg yolk off his chin, as he looked around, hoping to catch a glimpse of the mystery chief.

Neuman slowly stopped chewing, his curiosity getting the best of him. "What kinda questions?"

Farley was wound up tighter than a spring, his words gushing out fast and furious. "Things like, who is, where was, when did...you know, spook shit, man! Everybody's talking about him. How could you not know, Neuman?" His voice turned into a loud whisper. "Bet he's a nark, looking for dope and shit. Ya know?"

Farley made it easy to get under anyone's skin

just like a mountain tick, and he'd just burrowed his way under Neuman's. Venting an anger and nervousness that almost everyone on board was experiencing, Neuman threw the last piece of toast on the plate, then leaned across the table. "Look, Farley, all I know is that Koosman's dead, and we're bobbing around on this boat, in this cold-ass weather, waiting for the fuckin' Commies to make a move." He flopped back against the seat, pointing a finger at his shipmate. "And if he's a nark, asshole, you'd better hide your ditty bag, 'cause shit happens!"

Seaman Harold Prewett slid his stocky frame across the bench, pushing his food-laden tray along the table, after overhearing Neuman's comment. "Guess you guys haven't heard then."

Neuman and Farley looked at each other, then at Prewett. "Heard what?" they asked in unison.

"The Old Man got new orders. We're pullin' out and headin' for the Sea of Japan." He shook his head as he gulped down a mouthful of orange juice, then ran the back of his hand across his mouth. "It don't sound good at all."

Chapter Seven

La Perouse Strait - January 30

The task force steamed through the perilous waters of La Perouse Strait at 0930 hours. It wasn't unusual for the islands to experience fog, wind, and rain. The day was no exception. North of the American ships lay the chain of Kuril Islands, and to the south, Hokkaido, the northern most point of Japan. Prior to World War II, the Kurils were owned by Japan, in fact, it was from the Island of Iturup that they launched their attack against Pearl Harbor. But following the war, Japan was made to relinquish the Kurils to Russia.

Earlier that morning, at 0730 hours, a COD flight had screeched down onto the flight deck after its trip from Subic Bay in the Philippines. On board was a first class petty officer stationed at CINCPACFLEET, who had specific orders to hand deliver the officially sealed envelope to Lieutenant Commander Brad Simmons.

In the privacy of the EOD locker, Simmons leaned over Grant's shoulder, perusing the black and white photographs laid out in three rows on the desk, the latest views from the Blackbird.

"Can't see any change," Grant commented, running his hand over the photographs as he examined each one. "Troops and artillery are still positioned exactly as they were four days ago." He leaned back against the chair, clasping his hands behind his head.

Simmons came around from behind the chair, sitting on the edge of the desk. He brushed his hand down the side of his prematurely gray hair. "Look, I know I'm no SEAL, and this body ain't what it used to be, but I'll do whatever I can."

"Appreciate that, Brad. We'll find something for you to do...you can count on that." Grant reached for the cocoon, dragged it closer, then grabbed the .45, released the clip, checked it, and shoved it back. His fingers curled around the handle, his index finger resting against the trigger as he brought the .45 closer to his face. He stared at the weapon, when suddenly, a new-found energy coursed through his body, his mind and spirit revitalized. Whatever plan he came up with, whatever they decided to do, they had to do it today. Grant started for the door. "Brad, stay here while I find Chief..."

Just then the steel door 'clanged' and Adler came rushing in. He shot a quick look at Simmons. "Excuse me, sir," then he fixed his stare on Grant. "Just heard...the E-2 reported that a 'Bear' and two MIGS have shown up on radar. It looks like they took off from the air base in Kamchatka."

"Where's the *Bronson*?" Grant immediately asked, at the same time grabbing the headset.

"According to radar, she's about two clicks at our 180."

The *Bronson* was about 2,000 yards away from the *Preston*, directly off her fantail, and that was too far for Grant's liking. He acknowledged Adler's response with a nod. Although he was staring at Adler, he was, in fact, no longer seeing him, as his mind raced fast and furious. He held the headset against his ear, flipped the switch and waited.

"Mullins."

"Call Kodiak, Tony. Tell them they're to bring the *Bronson* in close, no more than one click at our three zero zero degrees, then hold her there. I'm gonna contact the *Bluefin* and ask Captain Stafford to start running interference between you and the Russians. He should have received his orders by now."

Mullins shook his head as he paced the control room. "Haven't seen the *Rachinski* since we hit the Straits. But the fog is pretty thick out there. I'll go up to the bridge and check the radar."

Adler was quiet but seemed to be asking: "What the fuck's happening?"

"At last check, she was off our port quarter," Grant responded as he looked across at Simmons. "Brad will stay here in the EOD locker. Contact him after you've talked to Kodiak and checked the 'scope. He'll know where to find me if necessary."

"You think this is it?" asked a concerned Agent Mullins.

"I think we're closer, my friend, but I'm still betting they'll wait till the fleet gets to Sado and we slow down."

"And what about you, Navy SEAL Stevens? You waitin', too?"

Grant couldn't keep from laughing. "N'yet."

"I didn't think so!"

Aboard the *Rachinski* - 0930

Sergei Vernichenko stared across the bow of the trawler, his deep-set, nearly black eyes squinting, trying to see through the dense mist. He spoke under his breath and only to himself. "What are you up to my American friends? What has brought you into these waters so suddenly? Surely, not us," he laughed without any true emotion.

"Comrade Vernichenko," called Communication's Officer Mikhail Borniski, as he pointed to the microphone. "It is Comrade Pratopapov."

Sergei walked over to the communication's table and tapped Borniski on the shoulder, motioning for him to leave. When he was alone, he sat in front of the microphone, hunching his broad shoulders over the table. "Has anything changed since our last conversation?"

"No. We're still proceeding to Sado. But..."

"But? You seem agitated, Comrade."

"There are many questions being asked."

One of the most respected but feared KGB officers in Moscow, Vernichenko was the best at what he did, especially when it came to mind games. Alexei had been an easy target, but now Sergei was very intrigued, the word 'worried' not yet crossing his thoughts. "You are being asked these questions?"

"No."

"Tell me about...these questions, and who is asking them."

Alexei spoke hurriedly. "The rumors have to do with a 'Stevens', Chief Grant Stevens. He's been asking about the crewman's death and..."

Alexei's words faded into the background as the KGB officer sent his own mind back in time, trying to remember. *There was an American--surely, it cannot be*. "You don't recognize that name, Comrade?"

"Stevens?" As if a bolt of lightning struck him, he gasped, "My God! How couldn't I remember?" He had been aboard the destroyer Hadley, stationed off the coast of Cuba, waiting for a sub to relinquish her passengers...five Navy SEALs, who were returning from a mission that destroyed the laboratory and nearly killed Vernichenko. Although Alexei had not been in contact with any of the SEALs, the scuttlebutt about what they did was the topic of conversation. An hour after the SEALs were picked up by the destroyer, they were helo-lifted from its deck.

But it was the KGB officer whose mind was flooded with thoughts and pictures of a time when the world hung on the brink of World War III--a nuclear war.

******

A revolution had taken place in Cuba, the regime of Batista overthrown by Fidel Castro. With Castro in power, Russia had its opportunity. The Russian Premier ordered a buildup of missiles in Cuba, and Russian naval vessels began transporting those missiles, bringing enough warheads that could literally wipe out the entire East Coast of the United States.

But while the Americans prepared for and anticipated a strike from the air, the first strike would, in fact, be coming from the sea, by torpedoes with nuclear warheads. They were small, two kiloton weapons, but classified as very dirty, "dirty" because of the massive amounts of radioactivity that would be released after detonation.

One of the most experienced submarine commanders, Sergei Vernichenko was selected to lead a team of scientists and weapons' experts in the development and design of two mini-subs with attached weapons platform for the sole purpose of delivering those torpedoes. The subs had two special batteries, each one capable of supplying power for a distance of forty miles.

Their plan was to launch the subs from the northernmost point in Cuba, head in a northeasterly direction and pick up the Gulf Stream, thereby enabling them to conserve power. They would follow the three knot current north until they were in range, then turn inland, one toward Miami, the other toward the American submarine base in Charleston, South Carolina.

All crewmen were volunteers, fully aware they were expendable, as the underwater shock would destroy the subs and them. Their mission was one-way; their sacrifice to be for the Motherland.

Seemingly hidden off an inland waterway, not far from the small town of Coralilio on Cuba's northern coast, the confiscated tobacco barn sat surrounded by tobacco fields and vacant shacks. Converted into a makeshift laboratory and research facility, the rear of the building was crudely redesigned to accommodate an office, kitchen and bunkroom. Electricity was provided by a small generator, shielded under a sloping overhang behind a propane gas tank on the east side. In order to provide some protection against dust for the laboratory equipment, a rough, uneven, concrete flooring had been poured in the main section of the barn. Long, stainless steel counters were positioned along the north and south walls with six steel, portable cabinets standing in a row to the right of the front door. Sitting on raised platforms in the middle of the room were the two mini-subs.

A dense moisture pervaded every crevice of the tobacco barn, saturating men and equipment. Cuba's sub-tropical climate was one the Russians were unfamiliar with, effecting them physically and mentally, sometimes to the point of lethargy. But each man was aware of Vernichenko's tolerance as being extremely limited when it came to complaints. Andre Mishenski, one of the scientists and the oldest of all the Russians, assumed the role of mediator. A long-time friend of Vernichenko's family, he knew the quirks and boiling point of the officer, having an uncanny ability to neutralize Vernichenko.

Vernichenko and Nikolay Soraovich, second in command, were in the office, located in the rear of the barn, adjacent to the bunkroom and garage. The two men were discussing test plans for the following day. Three sets of blueprints were spread out on an improvised wooden desk made of barn planks, both men leaning under the harsh, exposed light bulb. Above them, tacked to the notched, irregular wall, was a yellowing map with an enlarged area of the Southeast Coast of the United States.

Only average in height, it was Vernichenko's great bulk and low-pitched voice that made everyone sit up and pay attention. "Go get the other blueprint," he ordered.

"Yes, sir," Soraovich answered, as he straightened up, pressing his hand against his lower back, feeling the perspiration bleeding through his shirt. The air whistled through the space between his front teeth as he sighed, "Ohh, another long night."

"Are you complaining, Lieutenant Soraovich?" Vernichenko asked without turning around.

"No, Commander!" Soraovich immediately regretted his innocent remark. His transfer to Cuba was a feather in the cap of his young career, especially being assigned to working on Vernichenko's project. He harshly reprimanded himself. His chest expanded as he stepped through the doorway into the garage, and he breathed in the odor of tobacco, the barn wood permeated with it. He'd been without a Russian cigarette for five months, as long as he'd been on the project. The Commander forbid smoking anywhere near the facility. In five months, he'd been nowhere else but the facility, and his appetite for cigarettes had not diminished. He walked toward the dust-covered Land Rover. The beam from his flashlight shone through the vehicle's rear window, a beacon of light searching for another blueprint.

At precisely 2230 hours, a tremendous explosion sent a fireball skyward, disintegrating the entire north corner of the building, the noise deafening. A satchel charge, expertly placed, detonated the propane gas tank. Orange flames quickly engulfed the dry wood, consuming it as if it were mere paper, spreading rapidly across the ceiling and back wall. Two scientists and one lab technician were killed instantly; both Vernichenko and Soraovich were knocked to the ground.

Within seconds, five men, prepared for CQB (close quarter battle), burst through the front door. They were dressed completely in black, with hoods over their faces, only their eyes exposed. The unanticipated event, precisely coordinated, prevented any sort of self-defense by the Russians.

Instantly, the staccato sound of machine guns ruptured the air, with bullets from the Uzi's spraying the entire building haphazardly, screams being cut short as bullets ripped into bodies.

Vernichenko crawled on his hands and knees, scurrying across the floor like a frightened crab, blood oozing from his forehead. Soraovich ran to him, trying to scream, "Commander!" but he was choking from the fumes and dust. He tried helping the injured officer to his feet, but Vernichenko angrily pushed him aside, bracing himself against the door frame. Crouching low, he shot a quick look at the storage chest where the rifles were stored, but it was too late. Flames were already devouring the dry wood. "Andre!" he called under his breath, knowing it was too late for all the men.

Falon, "tail-end Charlie", the shortest of the SEALs, swept the area with his helmet camera, rushing over to one of the mini-subs, shooting pictures of the instrument panel and weapons platform, smoke beginning to cloud the view.

Ensign Grant Stevens shouted, "Grab all the intel you can! And rip-search those bodies!"

Four men immediately put the orders into action, slicing the uniforms from the dead with their K-bars in one swift motion from crotch to neck. The clothes were pulled from the bodies, wadded up, then stuffed inside the SEALs' utility vests, all in a matter of seconds.

Still unnoticed because of the flames and smoke, Vernichenko grabbed Nikolay's shirt-sleeve, dragging the dumbfounded officer toward the Land Rover, glancing over his shoulder at the burning maps and blueprints. A fire, burning as hot and furious as the one consuming the barn, raged in Vernichenko. *All our work.* But it was the loss of his old friend, Andre, that caused an uncommon pain deep within him. He angrily whispered, "I will never forget...never."

Grant tried to make a quick body count through the smoke and debris, his flashlight as useless as high beams in a dense fog. "Oh, Christ! There's only nine!" They all snapped around when hearing the noise from the Land Rover's engine. With the blazing fire cutting off their path to the garage, the SEALs raced from the inferno through the door.

"Rusty! Blake! Set the charges!" Grant yelled over his shoulder before disappearing around the corner of the building. With Falon and Ellis in hot pursuit, they sprinted at full speed toward the rear of the barn. Charred pieces of shredded roof fell around them as they hurdled debris and the bodies of two guards.

With its engine screaming, the Land Rover smashed through the wall, its rearend fishtailing on the soft earth. The SEALs were forced backward, and for one split second, the contorted face of Sergei Vernichenko glared at them from behind the steering wheel.

Machine gun fire erupted, a stream of bullets punching holes in the vehicle, blowing out the side and back windows. Nikolay Suraovich slumped toward the driver's seat, then his body slammed back against the passenger's door as the vehicle veered left, cutting across the tobacco field.

Grant, Falon and Ellis ran at top speed after the Rover, never releasing the Uzi triggers. The vehicle went airborne when it hit a knoll, traveling nearly 50 feet before landing on the other side. With dust and smoke trailing, it disappeared from view. "Goddamnit! Anyone else get a look at those guys?" Grant yelled.

Falon nodded and replied, "Yeah, got a snapshot, skipper," as he pointed to his helmet camera.

"Let's get the hell outta here!" Grant ordered.

Three satchel charges, one set at each corner of the building, exploded in an illusion of organized chaos. A brilliant white glow lit up the field, raining flames on the shriveled tobacco leaves, setting off numerous small fires. With the wooden corner support gone, the remainder of the roof crumbled inside itself.

The five Navy SEALs' mission had been completed, and, as quickly and silently as they had come, they vanished into the field, hustling to make their way back to the inland waterway.

******

"Comrade Vernichenko?" called Alexei after getting no response.

"Yes, yes, go on," he answered brusquely. Rubbing his forehead, Vernichenko momentarily felt the same anger he felt that fateful day.

"I kept trying to find out about him without raising suspicion, but it was like he didn't exist." Alexei shook his head. "Now I understand why."

Yes, it's like they don't exist until they want you to know, and then...it is too late. Vernichenko leaned toward the microphone, thinking that an old nemesis might once again interfere with his country's strategy. He sensed Alexei's growing apprehension. "Remember, Comrade, all your years of waiting to help Mother Russia will culminate tonight. We must be very wary. You must keep an ever-present vigil now. Proceed with caution, but continue as planned. This time we will not fail."

Preston - 0950 hours

From the first conversation between the Russians that he'd intercepted, there was something that gnawed away at Grant Stevens' brain. It happened again when he and Adler sent the MSV to the trawler.

As he and Adler were inspecting their diving gear--masks, hoses, and breathing apparatus--Grant was thinking about sending a message to Captain Stafford. As quickly as the thought passed through his mind, another nearly brought him out of the chair. "Christ!"

Adler looked up and casually replied, "You called, sir?"

Grant laughed. "I've got a bad case of rectalencephalitis, Joe." He grabbed the headphones and adjusted the radio frequency. Within seconds, he heard, "Admiral Morelli's office."

"Gardner? This is Commander Stevens. I need to talk with the Admiral--ASAP!"

"Hold a minute, sir, he's right here."

"Grant! Something happen?" Morelli asked as he dropped his coat over the back of the chair in the outer office.

"Not yet, sir, but I need you to get me some information. Put me on scramble, sir."

"Speak...I'm listening." Morelli motioned for

Gardner to hand him a pencil.

"I'll give you a few names. Can you match them up against the men stationed aboard the HADLEY and the sub during October, '62?"

"During the Cuban crisis?" Morelli asked with surprise.

Grant cleared his throat. "Yes, sir. It's just a hunch, but if I'm right, we're one big step closer to nailing his ass, sir."

"Good Christ! Give me the names." Morelli shook his head each time he wrote down a name. With the information on paper, he dropped the pencil and handed the list to Gardner, pointing with his finger toward the door. Gardner didn't waste time and ran down the hallway. "We'll get on it immediately, then will call you."

"Lieutenant Commander Simmons, Chief Adler or I will be here, sir. And Admiral...thanks for getting us the extra time. We're working as fast as we can, sir."

Morelli's tone sounded like a father answering a son, "I know you are, Grant."

Adler unlocked the door after hearing the tapping. Brad Simmons' expression immediately caught the attention of the two men.

"What is it?" asked Grant as he switched off the radio.

"They're getting ready to ship the Koosman kid's body, if this fog clears. Helo's going to fly him to the big island, Honsho, drop him off at Yokota Air Force Base, and then take him to the States."

Grant walked toward the bunks with his head

lowered, his hands in his back pockets. His voice sounded weary. "Do you know where he was from?"

"I think Washington State."

"Damn it! What a waste." He dropped down on the bunk, running his hand in frustration over the top of his head.

Joe Adler immediately interpreted the look on Grant's face. "You've been running your ass off since you've come aboard, sir. Don't know what else you could've done. This one wasn't yours, sir."

Grant shook his head, a fixed, fiery stare burned in his eyes. The square jaw clenched tight, until the muscles twitched as he bit down hard on his teeth. Adler's eyes narrowed, watching 'Panther'. He knew the look. Some sad-sack mother was gonna bite the bullet sooner or later. He walked in front of Grant, stood at attention and said quietly under his breath, "It's time to dance, Commander. I'm here if you need me."

Grant looked up with acknowledgment and something that resembled a grin. "I know you will be, 'Big A'. I never questioned that."

A boson's pipe was heard over the loudspeaker, sounding for everyone's attention. "All hands, listen up. This is the Captain. Replenishing at sea will commence at 1300 hours with the Suribachi. Deck force, make preparations and have on my desk by 1100 hours for officers' call."

Grant paced in front of the desk with his hands thrust into his pockets. The loudspeaker seemed just a muffled noise somewhere in his mind. The Captain continued: "We're still proceeding to Sado. Our expected arrival time is approximately 1700 hours. I wish I could give you more on the present situation, but that's all I have at this time."

Grant sat on the edge of the desk, ignoring the broadcast, thinking out loud: "We're gonna have to take a chance." He took his pen from his shirt pocket, wrote his own form of encrypted note on the desk pad, then looked at Brad. "Can you set up infrared cameras in both Damage Control lockers, aiming them at the doors?" Once the special camera was activated, it would take a picture when the lens picked up any white or red light.

"Sure, no problem. Now?"

"Now." Brad started for the door when Grant added, "Watch yourself."

The door clanged shut and Adler skeptically asked, "You really think he'll use those lockers again after what happened?"

"We've gotta cover all bases." He rubbed the back of his neck, the muscles as tight as a mooring line. "And we have to consider he might have a backup, Joe."

"Oh, Christ! You don't think that's possible, do you?"

Grant shrugged his shoulders. "Who the hell knows?"

USS *Preston* - 1030

Simmons rolled the chair toward the desk, then

picked up the headphones. "Yes, Admiral, he's right here." He tossed the headphones to Grant.

"Grant here, Admiral. Any luck?"

"I've got two with last names that match what you gave me...an ensign on the Hadley, and a first class machinist mate on the sub. There was a first and last name match belonging to a weapons' officer on the HADLEY." Morelli held his breath as he waited for Grant's response.

"That's gotta be him, sir!"

"Oh, Christ! I didn't want to believe it. You're sure it's Donovan? Mike Donovan?"

"We should have positive confirmation soon, Admiral. I don't remember if I met him on the HADLEY. The Team stayed pretty much to itself after the ship picked us up."

Morelli chewed the tip of the Havana right off, spitting it across the desk. "Look, you get back to me with that confirmation. I'll wait here all night if I have to."

Grant grabbed his cap. "Brad, stay here in case the Admiral or Mullins call. Come on, Joe."

"Where to?" Adler asked as he reached on top of the shelf for his hat.

"I'm going to the bridge."

Adler stopped dead in his tracks. "You're going where?"

"I've got to force him to make a move. He has to know who I am by now...I want him to know. You stay out of sight then come and call me. I'll need an excuse to leave."

Ten minutes later, Grant walked onto the

bridge. Captain Donovan was sitting in his swivel chair, facing sideways toward the port window. The fog had all but dissipated, leaving water droplets on the glass. He rested his head against his palm as he read the message traffic board lying in his lap.

"Hey, Chief Stevens, isn't it?" CAG said loudly as he walked over to shake Grant's hand.

Out of the corner of his eye, Grant saw Donovan's head snap up, the chair start to turn, then stop. *Yeah, you bet your ass you know who I am.*

"You haven't met the captain," said CAG as he started toward the forward part of the bridge. "Captain, this is Chief Stevens."

"It's too bad we couldn't have met under better circumstances, Captain," Grant said. Donovan nodded in acknowledgment, but there was a visible slump to the shoulders as an ashen but hard face stared at Grant Stevens. He remained quiet, his vocal cords feeling as if they'd been severed.

"Excuse me, Captain," interrupted Joe Adler as he walked quickly across the bridge, "but Chief Stevens is needed down on deck two."

"Let's go, Chief. Hope we can talk again sometime, Captain." Grant gave somewhat of a salute and immediately rushed from the bridge. Donovan regained his composure, glaring into the back of Grant Stevens.

Once in the confinement of the EOD locker, Adler shut the door behind them. "Well, that seemed to go well!" he laughed, shaking his head.

Grant threw his cap on the bunk. "Now, we just

have to wait." He looked at his watch, then reached for his stash of Snickers bars in the desk drawer and tossed one to Adler. "If Brad's not back in thirty minutes, go check on him, Joe." Putting on the headset, he adjusted the radio frequency, hoping to pick up a transmission.

Fifty-five minutes later, there was a tapping at the EOD locker door, and a grinning Brad Simmons rushed in. Grant swung the chair around, pulling off the headset. "You got it...you got the fuckin' picture!"

"Damn straight, we did!"

Grant waited impatiently. Finally hearing the familiar voice, he said, "Admiral! Scramble this, sir."

Morelli hit the scramble button. "We're clear, Grant."

"I'm confirming, sir. It's Donovan."

Morelli slumped into his chair. "Good work, Grant, and to Lieutenant Commander Simmons and Senior Chief Adler, as well."

"Thanks, Admiral; I'll tell them. But we still don't know what they've got planned exactly, or when."

"I know, I know," answered a drained Morelli.

"Sir, we were able to get his picture when he entered the DC locker, which means he probably contacted the trawler from there." Grant heard a muffled "shit". "I'm sorry I wasn't able to pick up the transmission. Sir?"

"Go 'head," Grant.

"He knows who I am, sir."

"You sure?"

"No doubt. I went to the bridge--"

"You what?"

"I had to force his hand, Admiral. It was the only way I could get him to move." Grant waited a moment then asked, "What do you want me to do now, sir?"

Morelli knew exactly what Grant was asking. "That decision will have to come from higher up. Let me get back to you, say, by 1500 hours, your time."

Adler, Simmons, and Grant confined themselves to the EOD locker. Since flight ops were canceled until 2000 hours because of the replenishing exercise scheduled, the remaining EOD team members made themselves scarce.

While they waited, Grant sent a message to sub Captain Reggie Stafford, ensuring that the *Bluefin* stayed close to the *Bronson*. His next call went to Tony Mullins. "We found him, Tony. We found the mole."

"No shit? Who? Who the hell is it?"

"Captain Mike Donovan."

Mullins nearly choked, spitting Coke down the front of his green polo shirt. "You're fuckin' with me...right?"

Grant felt drained, but it had only just begun. "I'm serious as hell."

"Christ." Mullins asked the obvious. "Did you get orders from Washington?"

"We're waiting for Morelli to call. One of us will contact you. Listen, Captain Stafford is going to be hangin' close to you now."

Mullins shook his head. "Ya know, with all this fucking technology sitting on this ship, I'm still completely helpless. Why don't we just blow the bastards out of the water?"

Grant smiled. "You've got my vote. Unfortunately, Washington won't accept it. I don't know what they'll decide. Maybe they'll try and negotiate with the Russians and Chicoms, you know, dropping a word here and there like, 'we'll blow your asses off the planet before you can spit' kind of negotiations."

"That'd be the fastest way," agreed a laughing Mullins.

"I've gotta go. Washington is due to call. I might be seeing you soon, Mullins-san."

Except for the distinct, muffled sound of the ship's engines, there was dead silence in the EOD locker as Grant adjusted the headphones. "Yes, sir?"

"Grant..." Morelli took a deep breath. "You're to terminate...with prejudice."

Grant lowered his head, then looked up at Adler and Simmons, who were standing side-by-side, staring back at him. As much as he despised Donovan, despised his act, it was the uniform Grant now saw, a U.S. Navy uniform. "Yes, sir." He stood up, shoving the chair back. "Anything else, Admiral?"

"You're to notify Admiral Hewlett and the XO. The XO will assume command when the time comes. You may need to question him about anyone Donovan may have been close to and keep an eye on them, too."

"Very well, sir."

Morelli felt uneasy, hearing the change in Grant's voice. "Are you okay, Commander?"

"Just...tired, sir. What about the trawler, sir, the *Rachinski*."

"A decision hasn't been made whether to use the *Bronson*. Will need you as standby. Can you be ready to 'erase' it, make it look like an accident?"

Grant looked at Adler and winked. "It'd definitely be our pleasure, sir."

Morelli stood by the window; daybreak was still over two hours away. He turned when his office door opened, seeing PO Gardner carrying in a cup of steaming coffee, motioning for him to put it on the desk. "You've got your work cut out for you, Grant."

"Not to worry, Admiral. I've got excellent help." He pulled off his headphones and turned to Simmons. "Brad, I need you to contact Admiral Hewlett and XO Masters." Simmons moved closer, already guessing what his assignment was going to be. "You're to inform them about Donovan. I suggest you talk to them together. Maybe you can use the guise that you need more information for NIS Headquarters regarding Seaman Koosman. Try to find out if Donovan..." Grant cut himself off and grinned. "Hell, I don't need to tell you. You know the damn routine!"

Off the Island of Sado - 1900 hours

Steward Mindina placed a fresh pot of coffee on the table and adjusted the cup and napkin until they were positioned to his satisfaction. He turned to Donovan, who was standing by the open locker, buttoning his long-sleeve khaki shirt, thinking about his meeting on the bridge. "Will there be anything else, Captain?" Mindina asked as he removed the silver tray from the corner of the table. Receiving no answer, he took a step closer, then called louder, "Captain?"

Donovan turned his head, his expression more lifeless than a museum statue. "No, nothing." He slammed the metal locker door, the sound like a shotgun blast, startling Mindina. "You can go, Edward."

"Very well, sir," Mindina responded, his brown eyes wide with surprise. "Are you alright, Captain?" he asked, concerned.

"Yes, yes. On your way out, tell Private Johnson he's off duty till 2000 hours."

Mindina closed the cabin door and relayed the message to the Marine, standing rigidly at attention. Private Johnson acknowledged Mindina with a nod, unbuckled the holster, and wrapped the leather strap around the firearm as he started down the passageway.

Hidden in the shadows, one deck down, Grant

made certain the coast was clear, then climbed the ladder. The broken piece of antenna had been taped to the photograph. He slid the top half of the photograph under the door, then rapped his fist against the steel.

"Come!" Donovan responded angrily. When no one answered, he walked to the door, seeing the photograph. Cautiously opening the door, he swiveled his head, looking up and down the passageway, seeing no one. There was only the faint sound of voices coming from the bridge. He picked up the photograph, slammed the door, as beads of sweat formed on his brow, his mind becoming confused. He started walking to his desk, then stopped, lowering his eyes to stare again at the picture and the antenna tip stuck under the tape. Why hadn't they come for him? An answer to the question didn't seem to matter. He had to take care of Stevens and hope it would give them the time they needed.

Walking quickly to the safe next to the locker, he spun the dial several turns. He yanked a walkie-talkie taped to the underside of the top, thinking how easy they made things. A casual stroll past the Quarterdeck one evening, where a careless shore patrol officer left the device, made it easy to slip it into a pocket. Unlocking the porthole, he aimed the antenna toward the open sea.

KGB Officer Vernichenko answered immediately. "You have news for me, Comrade?"

Alexei's back straightened. "Yes, I have news," he answered as he glanced toward the desk. "I'm sure I've been discovered. They know who I am."

"How can you be sure?"

"Stevens and I had a brief meeting on the bridge earlier. Perhaps it was his arrogance, but I knew then." Alexei explained the photograph incident and where the picture was taken. "And I'm positive he's the one who left the photograph under my cabin door."

Vernichenko responded, "I've done my own checking on our friend 'Chief Stevens'. He's not a chief, but a commander, and he's not just a Navy SEAL. He's working for Washington with their Naval Investigative Service." Vernichenko sounded confident as he continued. "It's too late for them anyway. We're moving forward. Moscow is expecting us to carry out the original plan before daybreak. They weren't pleased we had to wait these extra hours." He sat back, staring up at the ceiling, taping his finger against his lips, thinking out loud. "That's why the Americans moved so suddenly into the Sea of Japan."

"I don't understand."

Sergei leaned forward, close to the microphone, his voice a snarling whisper. "You, my friend...it was because of you. With you as a suspect, they wanted to see what we would do...I'll stake my career on it."

"Then explain why I'm still in command?" Alexei shot back.

"Perhaps the photograph incident was to frighten you into making a mistake. After all, you have the right to inspect any area of the ship. You have master keys. How could they know your true reason for being in that room?" He paused a moment. "They must not have complete proof. But with their attention on you, our plan may be easier to carry out now."

Alexei was beginning to feel like a piece of bait, losing the importance of his original mission. "I assumed they--"

"You know we don't assume, Comrade," he said condescendingly. With his lips nearly touching the microphone, Vernichenko's tone was threatening. "And, Comrade, I advise you to avoid Stevens from now on. No personal agenda will be tolerated. You will not jeopardize our mission. Do you understand me?"

"Yes," answered Alexei, trying to disguise his anger, wondering if Vernichenko was psychic.

Vernichenko immediately said, "This will be our last transmission. Now, tell me, do you have the devices in place?"

"I've set them in the RAM Room and in after-steering. The hydraulic lines will be severed; the ship will be out of control." The RAM was the hydraulic system used for rudder control while after-steering had backup, manual control lines in case the bridge-to-steering became non-functional.

Vernichenko nodded approvingly. "That's good. At the crucial moment, you will set off the devices and your mission will be complete. We will meet soon, Comrade." He stood up and angrily slapped at the radio switch, ending the transmission.

The trawler lurched, throwing him sideways. He grabbed his black leather coat and went out on deck, balancing himself against the wheelhouse. A cold spray washed over the bow as the boat crashed into a wave. He wiped the water from his face, enjoying the harshness of the evening. "So, 'Captain Donovan', you have been discovered. Perhaps this is not so bad for us--but what about for you?" He smiled. A military man himself before joining the KGB, he believed in serving his country purely for the love of Russia. Alexei had been promised a very comfortable living once his assignment was completed, cutting against the grain of Vernichenko's ideals.

All the months of planning were soon to culminate. Whether Alexei Pratopapov survived was not critical. And he had not been given specific orders to ensure Alexei's survival. In his eyes, the mole was just a pawn being used for one purpose, and one purpose only--the *Bronson*'s technology. He stepped into the wheelhouse, the door slamming behind him. "Captain, change our course toward the American carrier," he ordered. He pointed to the young third officer standing next to the radar table. "You. Go below and tell First Officer Kiriatkin to meet me in my cabin in fifteen minutes. Tell him to prepare his equipment."

He went by the navigator and stared at the compass, thinking, *Comrade Pratopapov, in the meantime, I think I will give you a little gift--the body of Stevens.*

Chapter Eight

USS *Preston* - 2030 hours

Flight ops had been underway for the past thirty minutes, the sound of jet engines continuous. Adler walked into the EOD locker and unzipped his green jacket. "So, you come up with anything yet?" He dropped his jacket on the desk then pulled the chair closer.

Grant was stretched out on the bunk, staring at the ceiling. He turned over, propping himself up on an elbow. "Yeah, think so. But I'm gonna need your help again, Chief."

"Sure. No problem, sir."

Grant pushed himself off the bed, running his fingers through his hair. "We've gotta do it now, Joe, while flight ops are underway."

Twenty-five minutes later, Joe Adler walked onto the bridge, the red overhead lights giving the appearance of a photographer's dark room. Captain Donovan was leaning over the radar screen. Dean Morehouse stood near the doorway leading to the Roost.

"Hey, CAG, need to get some ordnance info from you about the F-14's for tonight's operation," Adler said loudly.

"Sure, Chief." The two men spoke for only five

minutes, Adler taking the conversation where he wanted it to go. "Appreciate your help, CAG. I tried to get Chief Stevens to come up here with me. Don't believe he's seen night ops from this level, but he's down in the aft hangar bay doing his ritual laps." That was it...Adler's assignment. Now, Grant could only wait and see if Captain Donovan made a move.

USS *Preston*'s Bridge

"XO!" Donovan bellowed.

"Sir!"

"You have the bridge. I'm going to the flight deck then grab something to eat."

"Aye, aye, Captain."

"Captain's off the bridge!" the boatswain's mate announced.

Donovan stopped by his cabin. He made a decision...he'd take care of Stevens, and screw what Vernichenko directed. There'd be no way for him to find out. Stevens' death would make it that much easier for him to carry out his plans and, ultimately, his own escape. His intention was to make Grant simply disappear, and what better way than into the depths of the Sea of Japan.

Hurriedly going to his locker, he reached on the top shelf, groping toward the back, then removed a deep, metal box. Laying it on the edge of the desk, he unlocked it. The Smith & Wesson .38 had only been fired at the practice range. His stare fixed on the gun as his thumb pressed each round into its chamber. He removed the leg holster and strapped it to his leg, secured the gun and pulled his pants leg down. As he straightened up, there was a brief glimpse of a reflection in the porthole, the face of a man who was one step closer to fulfilling his role, to becoming the Russian he was born to be. The lines around his eyes and creases in his forehead seemed much deeper, perhaps reflecting the depth of his commitment and dedication. He brushed away the beads of sweat along his temple, his hand as steady as a rock. He smiled briefly, then left the cabin.

Hangar Bay

Except for one Sea King chopper being checked for an oil leak and a Phantom with landing gear trouble, all other aircraft were up on the flight deck. The hangar bay was nearly empty.

Grant was into his sixth lap around the perimeter of the hangar bay, his Navy blue shorts and drab olive green undershirt showing dark, wet patches, perspiration dotted his brow. The rhythmic sound of his sneakers hitting the deck was but a distant sound somewhere in his mind, his concentration totally on his surroundings. Unseen beneath his undershirt was a smaller version of a K-bar, hanging upside down by a leather thong, making withdrawal easy and rapid. He'd learned the survival trick from his platoon commander on his first trip to Vietnam. The feel of the cool metal against his chest kept him focused.

He was just coming into the darkened area at the rear of the jet engine shop. Something that looked like a human figure caught his eye; he slipped his hand under his T-shirt, closing his fingers around the K-bar.

The after mooring line reels, six feet high and resembling giant bobbins, would be a good place for someone to hide. He stared harder, but a second later, whatever may have been there was gone. He withdrew his hand from under his shirt, instantly regretting his move...but it was too late.

"Hold it, Stevens!" Donovan said in a gruff whisper. Grant stopped short, seeing the outline of a gun in Donovan's hand as he remained in the shadows. Donovan backed up one step and again ordered, "Move over here with your hands behind your head." He motioned to his right with the gun. Grant took a couple of steps, moving closer to the bulkhead, both of them in the shadows, impossible to be seen by anyone in the hangar bay.

"So, Chief Stevens--"

Grant's inflection was meant to imply contempt. "It's 'Commander', Captain."

Donovan's voice was slightly muffled by the sound of the screaming engines of an Intruder taking off above them. "Thank you for reminding me, Commander. I'd just been informed of your true rank."

"You mean by Comrade Vernichenko?" Grant shot back.

"That's unimportant now. You succeeded in Cuba when you destroyed our laboratory, our plans, but I'm afraid you will not succeed this time."

The two men had only four feet separating them, Grant trying to inch his way closer. Dropping the military formality, he said, "You've gotta know I'm not the only one who's aware of you, Donovan...or do you prefer I use your real name?"

"It's Alexei, Alexei Pratopapov. And it doesn't matter who else knows. All this will soon be over. Right now I'm here to eliminate you, you who has been like a thorn in the side of Russia." There was a mocking tone in his voice, as he added, "A very small thorn, but still, an annoyance."

Grant was trying to buy some time. "Aren't you wondering why you haven't been thrown unceremoniously in the brig, Alexei? Aren't you the least bit curious?" He could detect a slight shake of Donovan's head. "No? Well, let me tell you anyway," he stated coldly and matter-of-factly, his voice deep. "We've got orders to terminate you...with prejudice."

There was a slight droop of the shoulders, the gun lowered just a fraction for a moment, but it was the moment Grant was anticipating. He had enough of the bullshit.

As quickly as a bolt of lightning strikes, his leg struck Donovan in the left shoulder, knocking him sideways. The gun's muzzle flashed, the sound reverberating in the hangar bay. Grant's body slammed backward into the bulkhead, the right side of his head feeling like it had exploded. He collapsed on the deck.

Hearing the shot, men working in the hangar bay came to a dead stop, unable to see into the darkened areas, until they saw a figure racing at full speed, slipping in and out of the shadows.

Donovan kept running without looking back. There was nothing left for him on the *Preston*, and it was impossible to go back to his cabin to get the remote control. He had to commandeer a helo and fly to the *Rachinski*. His mind was already plotting a story to tell Vernichenko in order to cover his ass. They'd have to come up with an alternate plan. There was still time.

"Stop! Captain Donovan!" Chief Adler jumped from the ladder. There was no sign of Grant, and after hearing the shot, Adler feared the worst.

Donovan ignored Adler's shouts and only quickened his pace. He jumped onto the third step of the metal ladder, nearly losing his balance just before he grabbed hold of the handrails, then he scrambled up to the next deck, knocking aside two stunned seamen in the process.

Adler yelled again, "Captain!"

Somewhere behind him he heard a shout. "Stop him, Joe!" He snapped his head around, seeing Grant staggering, blood running down the side of his face, motioning with his hand for Adler to keep going.

Donovan was running at full bore, his gun hand hanging by his side, his index finger loose around the trigger. He ran down the outer passageway then leaped through an open watertight door, bounding across the flight deck, focusing on a Marine chopper poised on the angle deck.

He didn't hear the warnings being shouted at him, paid no heed to the sound of the engines. Captain Donovan, a.k.a. Alexei Pratopapov, in an instant, disappeared into an F-14's right intake, his upper body ground to pieces like meat passing through a meat grinder.

The .38 clanged against the aircraft before dropping on the deck like a rock. The aircraft shook and vibrated as the turbine began breaking up. The pilot's face turned stark white. With a voice screaming in his headset, he immediately shut down, then he and his RIO scrambled out of the cockpit, running clear of the plane.

Grant caught up to Adler, resting his hand against the bulkhead, steadying himself. Both of them had seen it happen before, but still, they stared at the sight in disbelief. "Christ!" Grant muttered through clenched teeth.

CAG and Air Boss Dodson came running out of the Roost, leaning over the edge of the wing along the superstructure, momentarily stunned into silence. Dodson ran back inside the bridge yelling, "Cancel launches! Cancel launches!" Two F-14's, two A-6's and the E-2C were making their final approach; rescue choppers hovered close by. "Radio incoming flights and bring 'em in!"

Simmons and XO Masters peered down from Vultures' Row. Masters shouted over his shoulder to an ensign, "Get the Admiral and Doc Matthews!" Simmons came rushing down the superstructure's outside ladder with XO Masters close behind.

Adler turned toward Grant, staring into a pale face, the right side covered with blood. "You'd better sit down, sir." Grabbing hold of a blood-soaked shoulder, he forced Grant down to the deck. Grant nodded weakly, wiping blood away from his eye, briefly cradling his head with his hands.

Brad Simmons ran up to them. He sounded out of breath, mostly caused by shock. "Doc's on his way."

Grant's vision was blurred. He looked up and tried to focus on Masters. "You've got the bridge, XO."

Masters nodded, then made a beeline back up the ladder, hustling back to the bridge. He passed the word down to send emergency messages to the rest of the fleet. They were all to cut back on their speed and to stand by for further orders. As fast as the Communication's Office could do it, a scrambled message was sent to each ship's captain.

Doc Matthews knelt beside Grant, pulling a square piece of battle dressing from his bag, holding it against the wound, immediately issuing an order to the two corpsman. "Get him to sickbay."

On the stretcher, Grant felt as if his head was an erupting volcano. Fighting to ebb the flow of vomit slowly creeping up into his throat, he struggled to remain conscious. "Brad, contact...Admiral Morelli...right away, with confirmation."

"Will do, sir."

A half hour later, the XO and Admiral Hewlett made a search of Donovan's cabin. "Admiral!

Look at this!" Masters called as he opened the black leather box. He lifted out a strip of black velvet. Hewlett reached for the material, staring at the awards presented to Mike Donovan. Among them were Vietnam Campaign, Vietnam Service, Meritorious Service, Presidential Citation, Naval Commendation, and his Naval Aviator Wings. On the bottom of the box, hidden beneath the Navy ribbons was a Russian passport and official photo ID belonging to Alexei Pratopapov.

Admiral Hewlett handed the two items to Masters, total distress clearly showing on their faces. He turned slowly and went to the safe, reaching toward the back. He brought his 5'9" frame to its full height, running his hand across his receding hairline. "I think we'd better go to sickbay, XO, and check on Commander Stevens. But first I want Lieutenant Britley to report here on the double."

"Sir?"

Hewlett held out his hand, a small, black object resting in his palm. "We need EOD...now!"

Masters' blue eyes widened, "Oh, my God.

Sickbay - 2145 hours

The antiseptic smell of a ship's sickbay was no different than that of a hospital operating room. Brightly lit, the room's sterile atmosphere was distinctly noticeable with the abundance of glistening stainless steel equipment and white sheets that covered beds and examining tables. Medical supplies, drugs, operating equipment were methodically organized behind locked, glass-fronted cabinets.

"How ya feel, sir?" asked a concerned Joe Adler as he rolled the stool closer, noticing Grant's face was as colorless as the fluorescent lights shining above him.

Grant sat up, his legs dangling over the edge of the examining table. "Have one bitchin' headache, Joe," he said with a forced grin, as he gingerly touched the bandage just above his temple. "Feel like a real ass for letting it happen," he commented mostly to himself. He squinted, still unable to bring Adler into complete focus. "Was Morelli contacted?"

Adler nodded. "Admiral Hewlett spoke with him. He wants to hear from you as soon as you're able."

Grant started sliding off the table when Doc Matthews mustered alongside, placing a hand on Grant's shoulder. "Hold it, Commander, you shouldn't be up!"

"No offense, Doc, but I...don't have much use for hospitals." For an instant, there was an unmistakable change in his expression and eyes. Only Adler recognized it. "Excuse me for a minute," Grant muttered. On his way to the head, it took total concentration to keep himself walking in a straight line.

Adler watched him till the door closed, then he turned back to Matthews. "He was serious as a heart attack about that, Doc."

"What? You mean about hospitals?"

"Yeah." He stood up, anchoring his thumbs in his pockets, glancing at the closed door, then back at Matthews. "It was during his last trip to Nam. He'd been there five months when his wife, Jenny, came down with some kind of viral infection and was rushed to the base hospital. She was there for three days." Adler stared into the doctor's face. "She died before he could get home."

Grant opened the door and slowly walked back toward the two men. "I'd like to go back to the EOD locker with Chief Adler, Doc. Okay?"

The doctor scanned the chart, then clicked the top of his ballpoint pen and began making notations. "Well, Commander, you've got a bruised shoulder, a mild concussion and several stitches. Will it do me any good to tell you you've got to take it easy?"

"I hear ya, Doc." Grant put on the blood-stained T-shirt, pressing his leg against the bed to try and keep himself steady, hoping Doc Matthews didn't notice.

Matthews continued writing while he said, "No sleeping for eight hours and no sun for twelve hours." He looked up at Grant, pointing the pen at him. "Agreed?"

"Roger that, Doc."

"Commander Stevens, how the hell are you?" Admiral Hewlett interrupted as he walked through the doorway. Following close behind Hewlett were XO Masters and Lieutenant Britley. Adler jumped up, standing at attention. "At ease, Joseph," said Hewlett, motioning with his hand.

Adler's jaw tightened. Joseph? He smiled and nodded at Hewlett. "Admiral."

Grant's head was spinning like a whirlpool and he swore to himself. He leaned back against the examining table for support. "I've been better, Admiral."

Hewlett showed something of a smile. He removed his cap and brushed his hand briskly over his crew cut, salt and pepper hair. "I'll want a full report as soon as you can muster one, Commander."

"Very well, sir. I was just on my way back to the EOD locker to call Admiral Morelli on the sat uplink."

With a questioning look, Hewlett shifted his eyes to Doc Matthews. "You're releasing this man from sickbay?"

Matthews shrugged his shoulders and nodded, "Yes, sir. But if the commander wasn't in such good shape, I can guarantee he wouldn't be experiencing such a remarkable recovery."

Hewlett took a step closer to Grant. His astute observation told him Commander Stevens was in no physical condition to be released. More importantly, he was in no condition for what he was about to ask of him. "Commander, we found this in Captain Donovan's stateroom." He motioned to Britley.

Grant reached for the small remote control, shaking his head, knowing immediately what he was holding. The size of a pack of cigarettes, the remote ran off a preset frequency. There were two buttons, green for safety, and red for armed. On the side was a toggle switch that transmitted the deadly signal. "I should have seen something like this coming, Admiral. I should have known." He held it out towards Adler. "I can assure you, sir, we'll get on it immediately." He glanced at Britley. "John and his team will be assisting."

Hewlett stroked his chin, and with concern in his voice he asked, "Do we have to worry that there may be timers on whatever devices are out there, Commander?"

Grant looked at Adler for final confirmation, then back at the Admiral. "No, sir. That's a remote control detonator switch. It's the only way." He swallowed hard, suppressing the wave of nausea sweeping over him again. "Except...we don't know where or how many there are, sir."

Hewlett stared for a moment at Grant, then briefly at the small device. "I'll leave it in your hands, Commander."

Grant came to reasonable attention with somewhat of a slight list to port. "Yes, sir."

With Simmons and Britley leading the way, the four men made their way back to the EOD locker, with Adler hanging close off Grant's starboard quarter.

Once sealed behind the vault door, Grant cautiously pulled his blood-stained T-shirt over his head and threw it in the trash can. He slumped down on the bunk, scrunching a pillow behind him, then rested his head against it, resisting an unknown force that was attempting to slam his eyelids shut. Adler sat on the desk across from him, Simmons and Britley to his right. "John, you bring the sniffer box?" Grant finally asked.

The sniffer enabled the team to test for the presence of explosives. By holding a tube inside a compartment, a sample of the air would be taken, the needle on the unit recording anywhere from 0% to 1% parts per million.

"Never leave home without it," Britley grinned, while he hauled his stocky body over to the foot-locker.

"Good. We need to get it warmed up." Grant held his hand out with the remote in his palm.

Adler studied the unit, when his eyebrows shot up, his balled up fist hitting against nothing but air. "Ya know, sir, that looks similar to what we use with our cable line cutter."

The cable cutter was a small box with a minute amount of explosives inside. An open hook was on one end that was used to hang the box from a line or cable. Once the remote control set off the explosive charge, it would eject a blade that would cut through the line.

Grant sat up straighter. "Joe, I'd bet a buck the explosives are in the RAM room or after-steering."

"Good place to start, sir."

"Can you round up your team, John?" Britley nodded. "Joe will hit the RAM; you go to after-steering."

"On my way." He grabbed his cap off the desk, then two walkie-talkies from the cabinet. He stopped by the door. "I'll report back every fifteen minutes."

Adler slid off the desk and walked to the metal cabinet, asking over his shoulder, "Weren't you gonna call Morelli?"

"I'll wait till this is over. Joe, hand me one of those headsets, then you take off. Brad, go with the Chief. Check back in with me to make sure these units work, Joe," he said holding up the headset.

Five minutes later, Grant responded to Adler, "You on low band, Chief?"

"Yes, sir. No one is on this frequency. I've checked it out."

Grant fingered the mouth wire and single ear receiver. The tiny device was used by the Teams to talk during CQB situations and other forced entry and clandestine operations. "Joe, where are you?"

"On the third deck, sir, midships." His stride was long, as he wove in and out of sailors and equipment on his way down to the fifth deck, the location of the RAM room.

"Okay, Chief. Talk to me again when you get to the RAM."

Adler started cantering down the passageway with Simmons staying close. "Wait, sir! How about the boiler rooms?"

Grant shook his head. "Don't think so, Chief. Since the CO did this, it would have been hard for him to get around down there without being recognized."

"Right. How about the weapons area?" Adler

immediately answered himself, "Hell, no. Not while he was on board."

"Check the RAM, Chief. Right now that seems to be the most logical."

"Back to ya later, sir."

Grant slouched down in the chair, resting his throbbing head against the padded backrest while he waited for Mullins to answer. "Tony, can only talk briefly."

Mullins swallowed a mouthful of Coke. "What's goin' down? Get your orders?"

"Captain Mike Donovan, a.k.a. Alexei Pratopapov. It's over for him."

"Jesus! This is unbelievable. I bet they're ready to fry his ass without even a court martial."

"No can do, buddy. His ass is already fried."

Mullins sat down in what looked like slow motion. "What...? I'm listening, Grant."

"The order came back to terminate with prejudice. I forced his hand, tried to draw him out, and we had a run-in down in the hangar bay. The bastard nailed me first, unfortunately."

"Hold it! You mean you're not in one piece?"

"Still got all my body parts, except for missing a piece of scalp. Anyway, he took off and ran onto the flight deck right during flight ops, and--"

"Oh, man, don't tell me. He didn't get caught up in an intake, did he?"

Grant nodded and let out an extended exhale. "Yeah. You guessed it."

"Jesus," Mullins said quietly.

"XO Masters has assumed command." Grant

pushed himself upright, feeling dizzy and nauseous, but mostly feeling pissed for getting himself into the situation to begin with. "There's more." He explained about the remote control and the places the EOD team was searching. "Tony, once the units are removed, the Chief and I are going to pay you a visit. You're still number one in the Russkies' playbook, whatever the hell that plan is. I'm positive no one else here in the fleet is involved and with Donovan out of the way, I think we'll be more effective from there."

"Think you're right. But are you up for this?"

"Have to be."

Mullins tried to lighten the moment and immediately added, "Tell ya what...I'll milk ol' Bessie out back then bake some chocolate cookies."

That got an immediate laugh from Grant, unfortunately, it also made his head throb even more; he squeezed his eyes shut and pressed his fingers against the lids. "Sounds good. In the meantime, call Kodiak and request they bring you closer, say within one click. The Chief and I should be able to hold our breath that long!" he joked. "Position her off our starboard side. We'll be departing from port, hoping to keep Ivan from seeing the helo lowering us. Will call before we lift off. And, listen, Tony, I think we may have a link higher up, too." Grant closed his eyes and swallowed hard. "Still thinking it out right now, but what I know is that Donovan or Vernichenko had to have an uplink in higher places. You copy?"

"Uh, yeah. I copy. Between you and me,

right?"

"Right, Mountain Man."

"Christ, Grant! You're some party crasher! Be seeing ya!"

Grant switched off. Now, he just had to wait for Adler. It was all too quiet in the locker, and with the steady drone of the carrier's engines sounding in his ears, falling asleep would be all too easy. "Get up, Stevens, you've gotta keep moving."

He lost count of the number of times he'd went from one end of the room to the other, but his thoughts were in constant motion. Something just didn't jive. Why did he have the feeling this was deeper than what he already knew? He went back to thinking about Donovan. He must have planned a way to get off the ship. How? And what was supposed to happen if and when the steering lines were cut? Was it just to be a way to slow the fleet down? Donovan had run to the flight deck, probably to commandeer a helo, but that couldn't have been the planned escape. Somewhere from the back of Grant's mind he drew out the night he and Adler used the MSV. He stopped dead in his tracks. "Shit! He was gonna go over the side through the outcroppings, lifeboat and all!" Just then his headset sounded. "Talk to me, Joe."

"Sir! We found the damn things! RAM Room and after-steering, sir!"

"Good work, Chief. Can you handle them?"

"Yes, sir. Lieutenant Britley will take care of after-steering. It shouldn't take long."

Grant continued his pacing, waiting for Adler's

return. Finally, the locker door opened. "Done, sir," Adler grinned broadly. He dropped his gear next to the bunks and then his headset on the desk.

"Good work, Joe, but give me a blow-by-blow later. I'm gonna shower then call Morelli." He looked at the door again as he started stripping off his Navy shorts. "Where are Brad and John?"

"On the way back here the XO sent someone after Commander Simmons. He reported to the bridge. Lieutenant Britley and his men were gonna finish with cleanup then make a sweep with the sniffer, just in case."

Ten minutes later, after showering and changing into his sweatpants, Grant was on the phone with Morelli. "Yes, sir. I'm okay, Admiral, at least nothing that a few bottles of pain killers won't cure." Adler put two aspirins and a glass of water on the desk, smiling to himself, knowing how much 'Panther' despised taking pills.

In the silence of his office, Morelli sat rigidly in his swivel chair, staring out the window with Grant's voice in the background explaining about the RAM and after-steering devices.

Adler opened the door for the Executive Officer. Masters dropped the passport and ID on the desk. Grant opened the passport, staring at a man who had led two lives. He told Morelli about the two items, finally saying, "I guess these put the final period on the chapter of Mike Donovan, Admiral."

"Except for the hearing and paperwork,

Grant...and we still have the *Rachinski* to worry about."

"Has a decision been reached on that issue, sir?"

"I expect an answer any time." Morelli reached for a cigar from the hand-crafted walnut humidor. He rolled the cigar between his fingers, staring at the paper band before biting off the tip of the cigar. Concerned about Grant's physical condition, he asked, "Are you going to be capable of carrying out whatever orders come back?"

"No problem, sir." He could only hope that wasn't a lie. "Admiral, I don't think we should wait for the Russians to make a move. Senior Chief Adler and I are going aboard the *Bronson*. I've already notified Agent Mullins."

"Whatever you think is best, Grant. I probably don't have to caution you, but don't jeopardize this assignment...or yourself."

When Grant took off the headphones, Masters was on his way to the door. He turned halfway around. "If you don't need me anymore, Commander, I'll get back to the bridge."

Grant eased himself slowly off the chair. "You've got a lot to do, XO. Thanks for your help." The two officers saluted one another, then Masters rushed from the locker.

Adler started to unbutton his shirt, until Grant said, "Don't get too comfortable, Joe, we're shifting over to the *Bronson* soon. Talked with Mullins, and he's making preparations."

Adler stepped closer to him, a concerned look

on his face as he scrutinized Grant's eyes. "You don't look so good, sir. You sure you wanna do this?"

Grant maneuvered around him and slowly walked over to the mirror above the small sink. "I don't see us having much of a choice, Joe."

Leaning closer to the mirror, he raised the corner of the bandage, inspecting the fine, black threads of the stitches where a patch of brown hair used to be. He flinched when he yanked the dressing from his head, noticing the dried blood as he dropped it in the trash. He reached overhead and removed a Band-Aid from the medical kit then squeezed some antiseptic on it. "Joe, can you have a couple of your men get our diving gear together?" He turned seeing Adler nodding. "And we're gonna need the scooters. Next, request that the XO give us the use of a chopper. Tell him we need it standing by." He went to the closet and removed a clean khaki shirt and trousers from the hanger, each movement slow and cautious.

"Going somewhere, sir? I mean, shouldn't you be--"

"Thinking of changing rates, Joe?" Adler looked puzzled, his brow furrowing as Grant added, "You're sounding more and more like the Doc."

"I was only..."

"I know, and I appreciate your concern, but I'm feeling better." He patted Adler's shoulder. "We can't come to a standstill, 'cause you can bet your ass the Russkies aren't about to." He stared down at the floor a moment as he buttoned his shirt. "I've gotta think this out," he said while tying the laces of his Cordovan brown shoes. "I'm just going to the fantail and take in some air. I expect it'll be quiet since the XO canceled everything but breathing." He glanced across at Adler as he stuffed his shirttail into his trousers. "You've got your orders, Chief."

"Right on it, sir."

Zipping up his jacket, Grant shoved his hands into the side pockets and started walking aft. Stepping through the last watertight door, he looked beyond the darkness of the vast cavernous space and went to the fantail. He leaned against the edge of the port bulkhead, staring out at the ink-colored Sea of Japan. The moon intermittently disappeared behind threatening clouds, occasionally casting its light on the water off the port quarter of the carrier. All was quiet except for the sound of the carrier's screws, agitating the water into a white, foaming frenzy, leaving a distinct, trailing wake. He glanced overhead with the cold wind whipping around him, bringing with it a hint of high octane jet fuel. These were the same smells, the same quiet, the same darkness, reminding him of his Bolivian mission as he stood on the helo pad with his team, waiting for the helo to crank up. This was his life. All these things were part of his life. But tonight it wasn't the cold that sent a chill through his body.

His head ached. The throbbing wouldn't go away. He tried to revert to mental concentration by invoking his karate discipline and blotting the pain from his mind, while he turned and went back into the darkness, walking toward the forward bulkhead. The aroma of hydraulic fluid drew his attention to the winch, and he noticed a small puddle of liquid under the brake.

Sitting down heavily, he pressed his back against the bulkhead, wedging himself in behind the towing winch, then he pulled his knees in toward his chest. Hidden behind the intensity of his eyes was a mental imagery of a game plan he was attempting to piece together, a means for stopping the Russians.

Even though Donovan was out of the way and the explosives were disarmed, the *Rachinski* had no way of knowing that and they'd be proceeding with their plan. But he had to come up with an alternate plan, depending on whatever Washington approved. What was it Morelli said? Keep an eye on anyone Donovan may have been close to? He had already dismissed the notion there was anyone else in the task force to worry about. As disturbing as it was, his instinct told him it went a helluva lot deeper than that. Just how deep was the question. He rubbed his hand across his face, feeling the stubble. "Christ! You're turning to shit, Stevens."

Twenty-five minutes later a metallic clanking sound shook him from his concentration. He bent forward and glanced around the winch toward the fantail. The adrenaline shot through his body, sending additional pain into his head. "What the hell...?" A telescoping grapnel hook had anchored itself to the edge of the waterway at deck level. "Shit!" he whispered. "I don't need this now."

Instinctively, his hand shot down to the knife strapped to his leg. He knelt down and scooted backward into the shadows behind the winch, the razor-sharp, black knife blade pressed against his cheek. He froze in place, hardly breathing, straining to hear every sound. A faint squish of a wetsuit booty exuding water as its owner stepped onto the deck, put the exclamation mark on his suspicions.

The unknown commando, his silenced, stainless steel weapon at the ready, crept steadily and cautiously toward the winch that would be his first hiding place. He peered carefully around the winch and through the open door that Grant had not too long ago come through. Seeing no movement, the commando took his first step toward the side of the door, swiveling his head back and forth, checking every angle.

The moment he started for what was to be his second hiding place, Grant sprang out. He instantly grabbed the commando's Norinko 9mm with its silencer and shoved the weapon to the side. In less than the blink of an eye, with all the strength he could muster, Grant plunged the eight-inch steel blade upward into the assailant's chest, cutting through the wetsuit, through the flesh, right below the sternum. In a true 'sentry silencing' technique, he ripped in side to side several times. The sheer force of the attack drove the commando backward, Grant pushing his own body against the intruder until both fell hard on the deck, groans coming from both men.

For an instant, Grant felt as if he were going to pass out, the blackness closing around him. But his own survival prevailed, and with renewed strength he jammed his knee into the commando's groin, his hand pinning the weapon against the deck, pressure on the knife never easing. Blood began gushing from the wound, slowly beginning to seep into the porous wetsuit. Grant held his position until the would-be assassin stopped struggling, the body twitching before going completely limp, a prolonged gurgling sound escaping from his throat, the final breath leaving his body. Yanking his knife from the chest, Grant pushed himself away, falling on his butt. With his chest heaving, he rested his head against his knees for a moment, squeezing his eyes shut. When he looked up, he was staring at the body of a stranger, a stranger who Grant assumed had more than likely come to eliminate him, someone who did not have the intention of dying for his country.

He turned the Russian's head to the side and looked into a face streaked with dark hues of camouflage paint. The Russian didn't appear to be much older than him. There was a deep, jagged scar running down the left side of his cheek and another splitting his left eyebrow in half, both conjuring up visions in Grant's mind on the possible causes.

The hammer and sickle insignia carved into the

weightbelt's buckle drew his attention. He unbuckled it, then jerked it from beneath the heavy, muscular body. He perused the belt as he moved his hand up and down as if trying to determine its weight, a twisted smile showing on his lips. "This will come in handy."

Noticing a steady stream of blood rolling down the outside of the wetsuit, Grant knew what he had to do. "Gotta make him go away." He reached down and grabbed hold of the Russian's ankles, dragging the wetsuited body across the deck, leaving a dark blood-smeared trail. "It wasn't meant to be my turn, Russkie," he grunted under his breath. The wind swirled around him, his pants legs flapped against his legs. He stared down at the Russian before kneeling down and shoving the body under the footline and off the fantail. He leaned forward, his brown eyes focusing impassively on a sea being churned by massive screws, watching the body flopping around in the percolating, white-green water before finally disappearing.

He took a deep breath before bending down near the edge of the deck and picking up the telescoping hook, then he flung it out toward the open sea as if throwing a boomerang. Lying on his stomach, he leaned over the edge and cut the line attached to the fantail ladder, releasing the small, black rubber boat the Russian had attached there for his getaway. Grant didn't know it then, but with this one move he had guaranteed luck would remain on his side.

Feeling a stickiness between his fingers, he

held up his hand. It was something he was very familiar with. He turned, looking for a water source and then walked over to the water wash-down hose, used to wash salt off equipment. Holding his hand under the nozzle, he stared, somewhat mesmerized as the fresh water washed away the blood. He picked up the knife, rotating the blade back and forth under the water, then dried it on the side of his pants. He slipped it back into the sheath strapped to his leg. Pressing his thumb against the end of the hose, he aimed the strong spray against the dark, red stain, forcing it along the deck till the last drop washed over the edge.

When he got back to the EOD locker, he saw Adler kneeling on one knee in the middle of the room, arranging various IED materials. Scattered around him were batteries, tape, clips, wires and detonators. He looked up when Grant walked in, noticing his disheveled hair and clothes. "Uh, don't take this wrong, sir, but you sure look like shit. I'd advise you to stop thinking if this is..." He stood up and squinted his eyes, recognizing the dark red stain on the jacket, alarmed it might be Grant's. Then he saw the Norinko. "What...?" A heavy "thump" from the weightbelt dropping on the desk cut his words short. He picked it up, his expression changing instantly, mostly from confusion. "Where the hell did you get these? What the hell's going on, sir?" Adler shook his head as he examined the Russian's weapon. "Jesus! Now there're foreigners lookin' to zap you! You're one popular dude, sir!"

Grant collapsed on the edge of the bunk and threw his jacket on the floor. He squinted in pain as he rubbed his forehead. "Yeah...real popular."

Adler went to the desk and picked up the water and aspirins that Grant ignored earlier. "You'd better take these. So, you gonna tell me what happened?"

Grant leaned back gingerly against the wall and gave a shortened version of the incident. Staring down at the floor, he muttered, "Can't believe part of this scheme was for Donovan to do me in, Joe. It had to be a snap decision on his part. It had to be." He shook his head slowly. "I can't believe Vernichenko would have authorized him to do it, not as long as he was still needed to pull this thing off."

"Why send a commando then? Pretty risky, too, don't ya think, sir?"

Grant nodded. "Guess I was getting to be too much of a pain in the ass, Joe. He must have had a lot of faith in that guy, though." He mumbled under his breath, "Think my KGB buddy must still be carrying a grudge."

"Sir?"

"Remind to tell you sometime, Chief," he grinned. Then, as if the incident never happened, he changed the subject. "Now, fill me in."

Adler sat on the edge of the desk, confirming everything Grant had requested earlier. "The XO's secured a chopper for us. I asked that it be brought down to the hangar bay so we can load our gear." He glanced at his Benrus and tapped its face. "It should be out there." The radio sounded and Adler flipped the switch on, handing Grant the headphones.

"Commander," said Morelli in his official tone of voice, "you may not like this, but your orders are to capture the trawler, and if possible, with all hands intact, keeping them onboard. You're to transfer the mini-sub to the carrier. Once you've succeeded, the Commies will be told and the trawler will be steered to a location near Russian waters where it will be anchored. Russian and Chinese representatives will be "invited" to watch a demonstration of the *Bronson's* power, with an implied threat, of course." Morelli hesitated slightly before adding, "If you encounter problems, any problems, the final outcome will rest in your hands. Do you understand, Commander?"

"Yes, sir. Understood." There was a brief pause in the conversation before Grant spoke up. "Chief Adler and I are preparing to depart for the *Bronson*. Agent Mullins will be assisting us."

Aboard the *Rachinski*

Vernichenko looked at his watch and pressed his face to the porthole in the communication's office, trying to see through the blackness. His excitement grew with the anticipated return of Kiriatkin and the completion of another successful mission. His breath fogged up a small section of the glass and he wiped at it with the back of his fist.

He asked anxiously, "Is the signal still growing stronger?"

The radio operator pressed the earpiece against his ear, tilting his head, trying to pick up any change in the sound being emitted by the device on the raft. He answered with surprise, "It...it's growing weaker, sir."

Vernichenko spun around, his voice a deep, fierce roar. "Weaker?" The startled seaman nodded.

A tracking device had been attached to the motorized rubber raft that First Officer Anatoly Kiriatkin took to reach the *Preston*. Once Grant had cut it loose, it rode on the currents, eventually drifting into the wake of a Navy supply ship close to the stern. Tossed about, taking on water, it grew heavier, the surface pressure from the screws finally dragging it under.

Vernichenko was about to call the bridge to change course toward the raft, when suddenly, the seaman pulled the earpiece away, a look of disbelief on his young face. "It's gone, sir. The signal--it's no longer there."

Vernichenko's immediate thought was Kiriatkin had been lost at sea. He turned back to face the window. The commando would never receive the accolades for his brave act. A photo of First Officer Anatoly Kiriatkin passed through Vernichenko's mind. The tall, muscular, thirty-nine year-old officer had stood proudly on the trawler's deck in his black wetsuit, saluting before going over the side of the *Rachinski* and into the rubber raft. Knowing

Kiriatkin the way he did, he was astonished this could have happened.

Vernichenko reached for a pack of cigarettes, tapped the bottom, then withdraw one with his lips. The match flared, reflecting in the porthole's glass. He lit the cigarette, his thoughts quickly changing. Things should be easier for Alexei now with Stevens no longer there to annoy him. He smiled, raising the burning match toward the porthole as if in salute to Kiriatkin.

But the KGB officer was failing to adhere to his own guidelines--never assume.

CHAPTER NINE

USS *Preston* - Aft hangar bay - 2300 hours

Two EOD men shoved the gear toward the rear of the helo, sliding the two scooters in last. The scooters resembled small bombs, eight inches across and two and a half feet long. They each had watertight electric motors and batteries, with a small protected propeller in the rear. A handle was attached to both port and starboard rear fins. Similar to a motorcycle's operation, rotating the handles forward or back determined whether the scooter dove or headed for the surface.

"You're all set, Chief, Commander!" Brockton yelled above the sound of rotating blades as he pointed inside the helo. "And the scooters checked out."

"Okay, Jerry," Adler nodded. "You two get back to the locker."

The men saluted Grant, then ran aft to the locker. Grant and Adler stood next to the Sea King, dressed out in drysuits, their face masks hanging around their necks.

Grant turned to Simmons. "Brad, call Mullins and tell him to ask Kodiak to bring the *Bronson's* speed to under five knots. Then, call Admiral Morelli. Let him know we're on our way. I'll contact him once we're settled."

"Good luck!" Simmons nodded then reached for Grant's hand, then Adler's.

The elevator rose to the level of the flight deck. The helo pilot brought the engines to full power, the sound continuing to disrupt an unusual silence. The Sea King lifted off the deck with its two passengers leaning out of the opening, scrutinizing the carrier's flight deck, an absence of activity painting an eerie picture. They noticed, also, that the F-14 in which Donovan perished had been taken to the forward elevator and brought down to the hangar bay. Grant's thoughts went to the pilot of that ill-fated plane, and he shook his head. "CAG's gotta get that guy flying soon, Joe." Adler agreed.

Once clear of the port side angle deck, the helo dipped closer to the water, hovering in place while a scooter was lowered, with Adler hanging on from the cable above it. Grant followed the same procedure. The backwash from the helo's blades and light sea chop tossed both men and equipment around in the water. Finally, a cable was attached to the cocoons, lowering them to within reaching distance. Grant looked up at the pilot and signaled him with a thumb's up. Attaching the cocoons to their utility belts, they started the motors of the underwater scooters, waiting for the carrier to pass. Then, they put the units into a shallow dive, running only ten feet below the surface, steering towards the *Bronson*.

USS *Bronson*

Tony Mullins stood at the stern, chewing a fresh piece of bubblegum. He raised the night vision binoculars. The *Rachinski*'s running lights showed it was positioned at one six five degrees off the *Bronson*. "Ah ha! There you are, you bastard!" Mullins stepped over to the port quarter looking for any sign of Grant and Adler. They'd instructed him to have two lines ready, each with a hangman's knot that was to be lowered to the waterline. He leaned over, seeing the ropes bouncing on top of the *Bronson's* eight knot wash. Just as he looked at his watch, there was a noticeable change in the sound of the engines. He smiled and shook his head, still amazed. Kodiak responded on schedule...the *Bronson* was now moving at a snail's pace.

Two dark forms began emerging from the sea, rising and falling on the waves. Mullins was tempted to shine the flashlight but remembered Grant said no extra lights. "Over here!" he yelled.

The two divers aimed their scooters toward his voice. Once next to the ship, Grant and Adler attached the cocoons to one of the ropes. "Pull it up," Grant yelled, "then drop the rope back down!"

They followed along with the scooters, until Mullins lowered the second rope, then they climbed the ropes after attaching a scooter to each one. Dropping over the side onto the deck, Grant immediately pulled off his mask and gloves, a smile on his face as he reached out, grabbing hold of Mullins' outstretched hand. "Tony! Great to finally meet you."

"You, too, Grant!"

"This is Chief Adler, my partner in crime," Grant said as he began hand-over-hand motions to haul up the scooter.

"Agent Mullins," Adler said with a nod.

"Please, call me Tony," he said as the two shook hands. Adler turned and started hauling the scooter up the side. "Here," said Mullins, "let me help." He grabbed the rope, then said over his shoulder, "Listen, before we go below, let me show you where our 'friends' are."

With the scooters stored at the stern, Mullins stood close to the rail, pointing with his finger and said, "There it is."

"Can I borrow your spy glasses?" Grant asked. Just the slight pressure of the binoculars pressing against his forehead sent a sharp pain across the back of his eyes. His vision blurred and he shook his head. "Goddamnit!"

Mullins looked questioningly at Adler, who shaped his hand to resemble a gun, then pointed to his head. Mullins nodded in understanding. "Hey, let's get the hell out of the cold, and I'll give you a personal tour after Kodiak winds this baby back up."

Aboard the *Rachinski*

Two Russian divers knelt beside the mini-sub, making final calculations, ensuring the battery was fully charged and finally, tightened the bolts holding the platform beneath the sub. The two jumped to attention at the sound of Vernichenko's voice.

"You're ready?"

Reznakov and Grimecko answered in unison, "We are, sir!"

"When you've finished here, come to my cabin and we'll discuss the details one last time."

At 2315 hours the three men were sitting around the wooden table examining the black and white sketches of the *Bronson*, drawn accurately to scale, each showing different angles. Vernichenko pointed to their objective. "You must ensure the safety of the microchip at all cost, even more so than the weapon itself." He put the cigarette to his mouth, taking a long drag, smoke streaming from his nostrils as he spoke. "The microchip and weapon are the most critical parts of the ship. With that technology, we'll be on equal ground with the Americans.

"You will neutralize the American on board, then wait for my signal. Then you'll immediately send an encoded message to the ship's command center, advising them of a course change." He pointed a finger at Resnakov. "You will stay aboard while Grimecko leaves in the sub. When you are close to the carrier, that's when you will set the self-destruct mechanism. There will be much confusion among the American ships, giving you time to pick up Alexei and come back here.

Once you've returned, we'll rendezvous with Commander Zeneski for transferring the chip and weapon." Vernichenko stood, both divers immediately jumping to attention. "Synchronize your watches. It's now 2330 hours. You'll leave the *Rachinski* at precisely 2345 hours." He gave each man a hard stare. "You have your orders." The divers snapped a rigid salute, then rushed from the cabin.

USS *Bronson*

Grant and Adler had changed into their fresh sweat clothes and strapped on their .45's. They unpacked the Uzi's and carried them along, instinct telling them to be prepared.

"This is still unbelievable," Grant said as they walked inside the bridge.

Going down to the 03 level, Mullins led them to his private mess hall and poured fresh, hot coffee into standard, white Navy cups. "Come on," he motioned, "and I'll show you SNAGS and the brainpower for this baby's weapon. Expect that's what the Russkie's are most interested in."

Up one level, the totally secured, watertight room was not what the two visitors imagined. The walls, deck and overhead were stainless steel. A sliding deck hatch responded to a coded signal from a small hand-held opener, not unlike a garage door opener, except the consequences would be extremely harsh if the wrong code was punched in. The unlucky individual would suddenly be holding a half pound of barastol explosive, instantly turning into thousands of pieces of flying shrapnel. Mullins removed the remote from his shirt pocket and pressed the accurate code. The hatch slid sideways like a pocket door.

"So, this is what our friends would like to get their sticky hands on," Grant remarked as he stepped through the sliding hatch opening, immediately walking to the SNAGS, examining and memorizing every detail. The small 'dish' sat on the rails that led up toward the overhead hatch.

Mullins led Grant and Adler to a control panel set against the port bulkhead in the room and pressed a black button recessed in the five-inches of steel. A 14"x24" panel lifted, revealing a small rectangular box. "This is it," he smiled. "Inside here is the chip that controls the weapon. This is what the Russkies are asking Santa Claus to bring 'em!" The controlling brain of SNAGS was one microchip, its prongs secured to the green 'mother board' located in the upright panel.

Grant and Adler leaned closer, Adler asking, "What would it take to remove..."

"Hold it!" Grant said in a hushed voice. "Did you hear something?" Instinctively, he and Adler snapped around and pointed their Uzi's toward the sound.

All heads turned as if trying to hone in on anything unusual. Mullins walked quietly to the open doorway, searching all angles down the passageway, then shook his head. "Seems clear." He went back to the panel. "You wanted to know how to remove this, Chief?" Adler nodded.

Grant's gut told him all was not right, and he moved closer to the door. Mullins pointed inside the panel. "There's a small clip behind this and you just pop the board out or pull the chip from the board."

"That's it?" Adler responded, surprised, while trying to get a closer look.

"That's it," Mullins replied, shrugging his shoulders. "Guess the masterminds figured the coded remote control door opener was enough."

Adler shook his head disapprovingly. "Always need a backup...right, sir?"

"You got that right, Joe," Grant answered, then quickly turned his attention back to the passageway.

"This is the backup," Mullins grinned. "Down in the computer and communications center there's the master chip sealed in a secure place. If anything happened to the master, this backup would kick in. Kodiak will receive a signal automatically. Come on, and I'll show you the center, the last stop on the tour, gentlemen," Mullins said as the door closed behind them. "It's my home-away-from-home."

Grant looked at his watch. "Okay, but then we've gotta get ready to move out," he said, cautiously looking up and down the passageway.

They went below to the next level. This time, all three stopped in their tracks, Grant and Adler bringing their Uzi's to the ready. They squatted down and scanned the passageways.

"Shit," Mullins whispered, as he reached for an empty holster, remembering he'd left it on the bridge when he went to wait for his visitors. He pointed to his empty holster, motioning to Grant he was going topside. Grant drew his .45 out of his shoulder holster and side-armed it to Mullins, never looking at him.

With their backs pressed against the bulkhead, Grant and Adler crept sideways along the passageway, looking into each crevice, whispering "clear" to each other to declare the areas searched and to let each other know where the other was. Both strained to distinguish where the sound was coming from. Mullins was on the opposite bulkhead, Grant's .45 in his hand, pressed against his cheek. He motioned for them to follow him to the Computer Center, figuring they'd have more protection once inside. He entered the code on the bulkhead panel, while Grant and Adler stood alongside, watching and listening.

First, Mullins crouched, then rushed into the compartment, covering the right side, then Adler entered, covering the center, sweeping his Uzi back and forth. Grant was nearly through when he heard the escape hatch open above them.

Glancing up, he saw a wetsuited Russian thrust his AK47 through the opening, no more than twenty feet above them. Grant dove behind the bulkhead as AK47 rounds chewed up the paint where he just stood. The noise from the firefight was earsplitting.

Grant and Adler rolled onto their backs and simultaneously returned fire at the hatch but it immediately slammed shut. Mullins scrambled behind the computer console, staring wide-eyed at the wires and cables hanging from the back. "Whoa! This is not a good place!" He crouched low, quickly moving out to the side. "Grant! There're extra Uzi clips behind you in the locker!" Grant heard him but didn't respond; his stare was glued to the hatch.

In the same moment he had called out, Mullins went completely pale, seeing the panel containing the master chip partially open. "Oh, Jesus! Grant! Cover me!" He scooted across the floor and punched in the code. "It's gone! Those bastards got the chip!" he yelled. In the confusion, he failed to notice the red light blinking on the console, the signal that Kodiak knew something had happened to the master chip. Now he raced for the console, calling Kodiak with a brief message.

Adler and Grant shot a glance toward Mullins, then at each other. Adler made a quick scan of the passageway, then shouted, "It's clear! Let's go! Let's go!" Without a word, the three of them scrambled up the bulkhead ladder. Grant reached the hatch first and a quick look assured him the Russians had vacated the area.

Seeing they were in a no-win situation, the tallest Russian commando called to his comrade, "Move, Reznakov! Back to our boat!" As they ran, Grimecko made a quick check that the chip was secure inside his wetsuit.

Within seconds both Russians had clambered

backwards through another compartment opening, pulling the hatch closed behind them. Grimecko took the butt of his rifle and hammered it into the control buttons, then he turned and raced to the fantail. Their final objective was to avoid being sucked into the *Bronson*'s churning screws. They reached under the footline and found the ropes hanging from the suction cups attached just below the waterway on the ship's main deck. Jamming the scuba mouthpieces into their mouths, they hung onto the lines and slid into the churning water just rear of the screws, the driving force of the water battering them around like rag dolls. They held on, literally, for dear life, as the rushing water forced them back toward the rudder.

Grimecko had set the side planes of the sub down two degrees causing it to stabilize at a depth of fifteen feet off the *Bronson*'s fantail, beyond the rudder. Now, they worked their way back down the line attached to the small sub, head first, hand-over-hand. Resnakov floated into the rear seat, feeling a sharp pain in his calf, and reaching down, touched a small bullet hole.

The sub lurched forward, Grimecko immediately steering hard to port, sending the sub into a dive, then leveling off at fifty feet. He bit down hard on his rubber mouthpiece, imagining what Vernichenko's reaction was going to be. They failed to complete their mission, never expecting to find three men aboard...three heavily armed men. There had not been enough time for them to try and contact Alexei, to signal him to set off the explosives. But they also had no way of knowing Alexei's fate.

Back on the *Bronson*, Grant and Adler raced topside, each of them heading for a different section of ship, trying to find any sign of the Russians. Grant ran aft and yelled "clear!" after checking the midships' passageway. Adler had gone forward and seeing nothing, headed aft, Mullins trying to catch up to him. The Russians disappeared, leaving only traces of blood droplets leading aft.

Gathering momentarily on the fantail, they looked at the wake and blood and knew that was how the Russians left. They moved topside to the bridge, Mullins the first to speak: "All I can say is that those two sure had some balls! Christ!"

Grant took his .45 from Mullins and slipped it behind his back, shoving it into his belt. He wondered how the hell the Russians knew the codes to get into the escape hatch and the computer center, and more importantly, the panel with the chip. Could Donovan have known? But Grant's nagging concern that there might be someone else higher up involved was turning into reality.

Adler stared fixedly at Grant's eyes, seeing the hunter/killer instinct that the SEAL had honed to a razor edge. "Sir?" he called. "Whatcha got on your mind?" He knew that somebody was going to be in deep shit.

Grant looked up, a scowl creasing his face. He walked toward the forward part of the bridge, his whole demeanor reminiscent of a pissed off cobra with a machine-gun. He turned back to face the two men. "The hunt's on again, guys. Somebody else is involved...and I smell meat." The term was used by combat-hardened SEALs denoting a fellow SEAL who "had been there, had taken no prisoners." He was known to his team as a "meat-eater."

Grant focused again on Mullins. "Tony, you contact Kodiak?"

"Yeah," he said out of breath. "They were ready to 'drop a cow'. I got them just in time." He slammed his fist against the bulkhead. "Fuck! I warned the Agency about something like this happening. Nobody wanted to listen!"

"Know what you mean, buddy," answered Grant nodding his head. "I voiced my opinion about putting SEALs onboard to back you up." Shifting gears, he got back on track. "Joe, suit up. Make a quick check of the outer hull and make sure those divers didn't leave any 'boomers' behind."

"Aye, aye, sir." Adler nodded and left immediately.

"Tony, call Kodiak back and ask them to bring the *Bronson* to a crawl so Joe can make his inspection. I'm gonna start getting our gear together."

"You're going after them, aren't you?" grinned Tony Mullins. Grant nodded, then gave a sideways motion with his head. Mullins took the hint. "I'm outta here," he said over his shoulder, leaving for the Communication's Center.

Friday, January 31 - 0200 hours

Adler and Mullins were on the stern transferring gear to a cocoon. Already changed into his drysuit, Grant was in the control center, winding up a conversation with Brad Simmons but not giving him all the specifics of what he had planned. "Brad, call Admiral Morelli on scramble with the details of what's happened and tell him we're going after the *Rachinski*."

"Will do. What time do you want that chopper?"

Grant looked at his watch. "Have it here at 0215 with the equipment I asked you to get." Simmons acknowledged, then Grant added, "Got to contact Captain Stafford. Talk with you later, Brad."

They had to move now, under cover of darkness and before the trawler could make a run for it, although, his gut feeling told him Vernichenko would get the chip off the *Rachinski*, probably onto a sub.

During the night the *Bluefin* rode closer to the surface, trailing an antenna, 'listening' for messages. She'd get one tonight that read: "Captain Stafford. Need your help. Must talk on secured line. Commander Stevens." Grant could only wait, knowing Stafford would have to break radio silence.

Within five minutes, he heard the familiar, deep

voice in his headset. "You looking for another ride?" Stafford laughed.

"Not this time, sir. We have a critical situation."

Stafford's back stiffened. "Talk to me, Grant."

"Sir, has your radar picked up a Russian sub in the area?"

"As a matter of fact, a Victor class was on the screen last night. We tracked it for awhile then it disappeared, that is, until two hours ago."

Grant's suspicions were confirmed. He and Stafford discussed plans, and as with their first meeting, timing was going to be everything. "Thank you, Captain. That's right...when you hear the signal, surface."

At 0215 hours the chopper was overhead, lowering a horse-collar. Grant ran down the starboard side toward the stern, just as Adler grabbed the cocoon. Grant immediately fastened a weapons' vest around Adler's arm. With a thumb's up, Adler slowly lifted off the deck.

Grant turned to Tony, grabbing his hand. "Wish us luck!"

Mullins shook his head in disbelief. "Man, I can't believe what you guys are gonna do!"

With a tight grin Grant replied, "Hey, that's why we get all the good duty stations!" The winch started hoisting him up as he shouted down at Mullins, "Get some more cookies ready for the party!"

The chopper increased power, climbing to an altitude of 20,000 feet. When they passed 15,000 feet, Grant and Adler went on O2. They checked the tanks again, adjusted the straps on the oxygen masks and finally inspected the chute. Their swim masks were in place, hanging around their necks. Last, they secured their 'hushpuppies', the silenced, stainless steel .45s that were water-tested. They shoved the .45s back into their chest holsters and fastened the Velcro strap.

The pilot shouted over his shoulder, "We're almost at the drop zone, sir! Standby for green light!"

Grant raised his hand in acknowledgment. "Here we go, Chief. Stand in the door."

Adler nodded his head. "Aye, aye, sir! If we've gotta finish it, this is as good a way as any!" A grin broke over his face and he looked at Grant. "Hey! Is this where we do that 'Geronimo' shit?"

The two were about to make a tandem rig, high altitude high open (HAHO) jump from 20,000 feet into an atmosphere with a temperature of twenty degrees below zero. HAHO's were a silent insertion technique designed to strike fear and confusion into an enemy, by drifting silently into their midst from the blackness above. They'd be breathing oxygen from a belt tank flowing into an aviator-style mask and would continue using it down to a breathable air level. They both instinctively cranked open the O2 bottle, then checked their face masks and tightened their crotch straps.

"Joe, inflate your vest at 3,000 feet."

"Roger that, sir!"

The green light came on overhead. They quickly exited the helo, Grant opening his chute almost immediately. As soon as he checked the tether lines and canopy, he nudged Adler and he released the stabo line used to drop a commando lower than the 'flyer'. Adler dropped twenty-five feet below Grant. The line was attached to Grant's chest straps, so both men were riding the same chute.

Their landing site was barely distinguishable, a speck of light in a vast sea, six miles away--the *Rachinski*. As they drifted silently, Grant got a quick fix on the still experimental GPS electronics package. He signaled Joe with a thumb's up as they drifted silently, then he checked the *Rachinski*'s course. She hadn't changed.

After passing 14,000 feet, they removed their oxygen masks, letting them hang from the tanks attached to the front of their belts. After Adler dropped off, Grant's plan was to land on the fantail of the *Rachinski*, just as they had trained on mock raids during Naval exercises. The difference this time was that Grant Stevens had every intention of being captured. It was the only way. The plan had to work or his ass would be in the wind.

At 3,000 feet Grant was maneuvering off the bow of the *Rachinski* and had a good head wind to keep aloft. At 1,500 feet they were forward of the starboard bow. With Adler hanging twenty-five feet below, just about at the level of the horizon, his detection was almost impossible when viewed from the trawler's bridge in the dead of night. And heavy, dark storm clouds rested against the horizon, making it a perfect night for the operation.

With one hand Adler held the magnetic pads tightly hanging from his utility belt by three foot pieces of rope. At twenty-five feet, he released the tether line. Legs together, head tucked in, life vest inflated, he hit the water heels first. He immediately popped up to the surface as the trawler started passing in front of him. With a swift motion, he pulled his swim mask up over his face, then cleared the water from it. With a couple of powerful kicks, he was at the trawler. He slammed the magnetic paddles against the trawler and holding on tight, he felt his body slide aft in the wake.

With the chute gliding down the starboard side, Grant swung inward. When he was about ten feet above the deck, he released the chest straps, and at four feet, pulled the leg straps' quick release and slipped out of the harness. He hit the deck and rolled to the side in a picture perfect PLF (Parachute Landing Fall). He instantly came up on one knee, raising his Uzi, anticipating a response.

And the response came within seconds. Armed Russians were running down both port and starboard sides of the trawler heading straight for him. The taller Russian yelled commands in Russian and then in broken English to Grant, ordering him to lay his weapon down, then to get to his feet.

As he raised his hands, Grant thought, *It's good to be home.* No doubt, the Russians were waiting for him. He was positive now...there had to be a leak in the chain of command, and a helluva lot deeper than he'd thought.

Five AK47s were pointed directly at him, the muzzles as close as four feet. With the rocking of the trawler, and with everyone trying to maintain their balance, it would have been easy to escape--but that was not in the immediate plan.

One of the guards shouted an order, and instantly, another cautiously walked toward the American and collected the 'hushpuppy' strapped to his chest. After handing it to one of his comrades, he returned to Grant, patting him down. Finding nothing, he shook his head, then returned to the ring of guards.

Grant smiled to himself, biting his tongue, not letting on he understood them. He glanced up when he saw movement on the afterdeck of the wheelhouse. The silhouetted figure stared at him for a long moment, his hands motionless behind his back. He started toward the ladder leading down to where the American was standing. Grant strained his eyes to give some substance to the silhouette approaching him, but he had a good idea who it was. As the Russian reached the bottom step, he looked at the American again. His slow, heavy footsteps pounded on the deck as he walked, stopping within two feet of Grant.

Sergei Vernichenko fixed his stare on him, a stare as cold and emotionless as a dead man's. He drew his arm from behind him and put his cigarette in his mouth, drawing in deeply. He studied Grant before bellowing in broken English, "Your name! Who are you?"

Grant couldn't let on who he was, not yet.

"Smith, Chief John Smith."

"And Chief John Smith, what could possibly bring you to the *Rachinski*...alone?"

Grant started to reach for the pouch on his utility belt, when one of the guard's shouted, "N'yet!" nudging his rifle into Grant's stomach.

"I came to deliver something to you," Grant said.

Vernichenko stood motionless, then gestured for the guard to back off. Grant reached inside, withdrew Donovan's Russian passport that was sealed in plastic and flipped it at Vernichenko, who showed no response, no emotion while he glanced at the photograph. Finally, he looked up at Grant. "So, you have captured Alexei. I suspected so after--"

Grant shook his head. "N'yet."

This time, Grant noticed a fleeting moment of surprise from the Russian. "So, you have disposed of him. He was careless." Trying to sound unconcerned, he added, "We were through with him anyway because he no longer fit into the remainder of our plans. You have done me a favor, Chief Smith."

"Do you want to fill me in on what was supposed to happen if we hadn't disarmed the line cutters he planted?" Grant asked as he tried to balance himself against the trawler's rocking motion.

Vernichenko pulled his shoulders back, staring hard at Grant. "With your steering capabilities gone, our commando was to set the timer of the self-destruct mechanism on the *Bronson*, then steer it into your angle deck, igniting your fuel and ordnance, destroying the *Bronson* and as much of the carrier as possible. You would have assumed it was just an unfortunate accident. And Alexei would have, shall we say, disappeared in the melee while, in fact, he was to be picked up by the commando."

"It appears your plans have been sidetracked," Grant said mockingly.

Vernichenko nodded, but then answered, "Perhaps we do not have your weapon, and your *Bronson* still prowls the ocean, but we do have what we were truly after...the microchip."

"You got the chip," Grant continued, searching for more information, "and we got our mole."

The Russian pointed a finger at Grant. "Ahhh, you must remember, just because you cut off the head of a snake peering from beneath the bush, you still do not know how far the body stretches."

That was all Grant needed--final confirmation. There was someone else involved. He glared into the Russian's eyes as he reached down and unfastened the weightbelt, hurling it against Vernichenko's feet. One of the guard's reacted instantly and rammed the butt of his rifle hard into Grant's right kidney, dropping him to his knees.

Vernichenko was distracted by the incident momentarily but said nothing. Then, he glanced down. His eyes narrowed, straining to focus on the belt. He reached down, taking hold of the buckle, the hammer and sickle insignia coming into the light. His head snapped up, the same anger rushing through him as that day in Cuba. He did not have a good feeling about this American.

Grant got up slowly, resting his hands on his knees, trying to catch his breath. He stared at the Russian before finally straightening up, already relishing the next few minutes. It was his turn to take over the controls. "We haven't been formally introduced...you are KGB Officer Vernichenko, I presume?"

Sergei stared at the American, a unusual chill running up his spine as he nodded. He leaned closer to Grant, then asked between clenched teeth, "And you are Smith?"

"I lied! My name's Stevens, Commander Grant Stevens, U.S. Navy."

The sound of the weightbelt slamming on the deck echoed across the trawler. A guard jumped aside as it narrowly missed his leg. Vernichenko's voice exploded. "N'yet! It can't be you!"

Grant's brown eyes flashed as he stared dead on into the KGB officer's face, taking a step forward, intentionally trying to provoke the Russian. "Believe it, friend!"

Vernichenko looked at Grant in disbelief, as an impression of his dead friend, Andre Mishenski, stood out clearly in his mind's eye. "It was you in Cuba...you who was responsible for the murder of my men!"

Grant shrugged his shoulders, his mouth turning up into a half smile. He was now playing the role of taunter, on the offensive, not letting up. His voice was intentionally loud, his Russian flawless. "Da. And would you like to know what happened to Alexei? Should I also describe my encounter with your would be assassin? Would you like to know what I did to his body?"

Veins stood out in Vernichenko's thick neck like tree roots rising from the earth. He bellowed, "Enough! I can assure you," he hissed, crushing the cigarette beneath the toe of his black boot, "this will be the last time we shall meet." He took a step closer to the American, a grim, unnatural look contorting his face. Each word sounded sharp and distinct. "We shall be rendezvousing with our submarine soon, Commander Stevens, for transferring the microchip." Eye-to-eye with Grant, he repeatedly poked his index finger into Grant's chest, leering at him. "And then, I think I will also transfer you to them...but only after I have finished with you! Do svidaniya, Commander Stevens, U.S. Navy!" He spun around and shouted to the guards, "Bring him forward!"

Grant silently scoffed, *Transfer my ass! Not in this lifetime, Russkie*!

The armed escort prodded him along the port side of the trawler, when the boat suddenly lurched. Unnoticed, Grant had the opportunity to loosen his sleeve. Two CIA developed MK36 impact smoke bombs, each the size of a quarter, slid into his palm.

Meanwhile, Adler had made his way to midships, planting an IED against the side of the trawler, setting the timer to four minutes. The mine had a magnetic face with a shaped charge inside. He crimped the chemical pencil attached to the charge. It contained acetone that would eat its way through a thin plastic washer. Once it did, the firing pin would ignite the detonator and the charge would cut through the three inch thick hull allowing sea water to come raging through the orifice, pouring into the engine room at 300 gallons a minute.

He was getting dangerously close to being caught up in the pull of the screws, but he continued moving further down the side. He planted another IED, this one closer to the screws, closer to the ordnance stowed beneath the deck used for the trawler's rear three inch deck gun. This timer was set for three minutes.

He pushed off and swam hard away from the trawler, stroking and kicking as fast as he could to escape being sucked under. Once clear, he turned, seeing the Russians with Grant ahead of them going forward toward the bow, his mind telling 'Panther' to hang on just a little longer. Swimming towards the port side rendezvous point, he set off his mini light for Grant's easy detection.

Grant was counting the minutes, anticipating that Adler would complete his work on schedule. Trying not to be conspicuous, he quickly scanned the water, seeing the mini light bobbing in the water. That was the signal!

He hurled the two bomblets, laced with chlorine and with contact fusing, onto the deck. Within the blink of an eye, he dove for the black water.

The instantaneous explosions released thick

smoke, engulfing the Russians. The caustic material burned the eyes and lungs of everyone on deck. A few involuntary bursts of AK47 rounds cracked the air.

Grant dolphin kicked hard to separate himself from the trawler's wake current and broke clear of its pull. As the force lessened, he surfaced about thirty feet away, the trawler's stern just passing him. He set off the tracking device attached to the inside of his sleeve.

"Commander! Over here!" yelled Adler.

Grant laid into the familiar frogman's kick, swimming long strokes toward Adler, knifing through the choppy water. They both looked up and saw the Russians, still in pain from the chlorine assault, some of them vomiting, others rubbing their eyes.

Grant spotted Vernichenko halfway up the ladder, leaning against the arm rail, wrenching violently. Nearly all of the chlorine cloud had disappeared. The KGB officer was desperately trying to find the American through the smoke and darkness. "Get that spotlight back here!" He jumped off the ladder and raced down the port side, hanging over the railing. The light found its mark. So intent on killing Grant, Vernichenko failed to put two and two together, not questioning the appearance of a second diver. "Shoot! Shoot!" The blinded guards fired aimlessly into the water off the stern.

Adler shouted, "I think we've really pissed them off, sir!" Bullets spewed erratically around the two

Americans, with the Russians being still partially blinded. "Shit!" Adler spat out.

Grant snapped his head around, toward his teammate. "What!"

Adler had his hand pressed against the front of his right shoulder. "Caught one in the same damn spot!"

Grant reached out and grabbed Adler's left arm, dragging him and shouting, "We're getting outta here! Hang on, Joe! We're goin' under!"

"Go!" Adler yelled back, sucking in a lungful of air laced with saltwater.

After swimming at a depth of fifteen feet for a minute, Adler signaled he was okay and Grant let go. Staying at a shallow depth, they swam as hard and as fast as they could for another minute. Adler's shoulder throbbed. The freezing water seeped into his suit. The strength in his arm was deteriorating, so he tucked his hand into his belt. His lungs ached and he pulled hard with his good arm, until he felt Grant take hold of it.

No longer hearing the staccato sound of AK47s or the 'zip' sound of bullets hitting water, the two Americans surfaced. Grant unbuckled his UDT life vest and slipped it over Adler's head, pulling it tightly around him. With the loss of blood and cold water seeping into Adler's suit through the bullet hole, Grant knew they didn't have much time. "Press it against your shoulder!"

He looked back, seeing the menacing shape of the *Rachinski* coming hard to port, powerful light beams splitting the night, guiding its way. "Goddamnit!"

"This isn't a good thing, sir!" Adler yelled.

Without warning, and less than fifty feet from them, the coal black sail of the SSN *Bluefin* slowly broke the water's surface, the red port navigation light coming into view.

Grant shouted, "Hang on, Chief!" He pulled Adler in a cross-body carry, sidestroking to the sub. *Yes, Captain Stafford; timing is everything!*

Stafford scurried through the hatch into the topside Conn, grabbing the 1MC and yelling, "Man the deck gun!" Six sailors poured out of the hatch, two of them ramming a 40mm gun into a deck mount while another slammed a full magazine into the top of the gun.

Aboard the *Rachinski*, Vernichenko had raced into the wheelhouse, his face distorted with anger, screaming at the helmsman, "Ram them! Kill the Americans!" The helmsman's face turned ashen. Jerking his head around, he fixed his stare on Captain Boris Belenko, waiting for confirmation.

"N'yet!" shouted the Captain defiantly, immediately barking his own orders. "Right full rudder!" The helmsman spun the wheel rapidly. Belenko turned sharply, confronting Vernichenko. "If we kill the Americans and ram the submarine, we will surely start a war. I will not do it, Comrade. I will not risk my boat and men for you or your mission! It is more important that we reach Captain Zeneski's submarine!"

Vernichenko grabbed the Captain's arm, crushing the uniform sleeve in his fingers. Pulling on

Belenko's arm as if trying to wrench it from the shoulder, he shouted, "Look around you. Who is to know?"

"You fool!" Belenko shouted, yanking his arm away from Vernichenko's grasp. "You know their submarine doesn't operate independently. By now someone knows where they are and what they're doing! Enough!" Vernichenko bristled. He was like a man gone mad, losing all sense of reasoning. His hand dropped to the handle of his pistol. Belenko lowered his stare to the KGB officer's pistol. "I can assure you that would be your death warrant, Comrade Vernichenko."

Two plumes of white water rose into the air, the shells fired from the *Bluefin* landing close to port midships of the trawler. "Look! Look!" Vernichenko swept his arm overhead. "You've been fired upon! You must defend yourself! Ram them!"

Captain Belenko shook his head, glaring into the reddened, angered face. Vernichenko knew he'd lost and rushed outside, racing down the port side toward the signal bridge. His knuckles turned stark white as his thick fingers curled around the rail, his mind imagining Commander Stevens' neck locked in his muscular grip. "N'yet! N'yet!" he shouted.

Two lifelines were thrown over the side of the sub into the choppy sea. Grant reached for a lifeline and quickly tied it under Adler's arms. He shouted up at the sailors hanging over the edge. "Pull him up! He's hit in the shoulder! Get him to sickbay!"

They pulled hard, reaching for Adler then quickly covering him with a blanket. Grant gave a quick glance over his shoulder as he grabbed the line. "Come on, goddamnit! Let's get it over with!"

For a couple of fleeting seconds, a muffled sound rumbled beneath the dark sea before the fantail of the *Rachinski* lifted from the water, erupting in a ball of fire. Smaller explosions immediately followed as flames devoured ordnance. The deck was awash in an orange-white glow, fire enveloping everything in its path. The inferno ignited fuel, hurling particles of ship metal and casings skyward and into the wheelhouse, shattering windows, striking bodies. With its screws destroyed, the trawler continued veering right out of control, smoke and flames beginning to surge throughout. A second charge ignited, opening a hole in the bulkhead, water pouring into the engine room. The trawler's list was unmistakable.

Grant was being pulled up the side of the sub. He rolled onto his back, staring at the trawler just as a final, violent explosion shook it, blowing away the remaining section of wheelhouse. The *Rachinski*'s starboard side was completely underwater, the port side just a smoldering, blackened shell. As if being sucked down by a giant vacuum, the trawler disappeared beneath the Sea of Japan. The *Rachinski* and all aboard ceased to exist beneath a bubbling, steam-filled sea.

And then there were none, Commander Stevens scoffed without remorse, remembering Cuba and the face of Sergei Vernichenko.

Chapter Ten

NIS Headquarters

Admiral Morelli stared down at the message on his desk, smoothing the edges with the back of his hand. The secured flash message was sent by Brad Simmons from the Communication's Center of the *Preston*, quoting Grant word for word: "Nothing to fear from the Bear or the Dragon. Put them to rest. Grant."

Petty Officer Gardner buzzed the intercom, reporting that Secretary Allington was on the line. Morelli picked up the phone as he looked around the office. During the past few days, the only time he'd left was to shower and change. His aide, Ensign Pritchard, had brought him his meals. His gaze stopped at the couch, staring at the pillow still crumpled against the armrest.

Allington cleared his throat, his voice sounding anxious, exhausted. "Admiral Morelli? You have any news?"

"Yes, Mr. Secretary. I just received word from Commander Stevens." He read Grant's message, then answered, "Yes, sir. Everything is under control. The incident's been defused. Once you resume conversations with the Chinese and Russians, Mr. Secretary, I'm certain they will not be taking any action. There shouldn't be anything more to worry about. The Commander will explain further when he returns."

USS *Preston*'s Flight Deck - January 31 - 0815 hours

Lieutenant Greg Connelly snapped a ready salute, and an instant later the AE-6B Prowler catapulted from the USS John *Preston*, beginning its long journey. Carrying spare external fuel tanks, the Prowler would be pushed to its limit since its mission was critical--deliver two passengers to Andrews Air Force Base.

Sitting in the rear seats behind the pilot and navigator, dressed in dark green flight suits and white helmets with red lightning bolts on the sides, were Grant Stevens and Joe Adler. The cramped quarters and long flight, with only one brief stop and three in-flight refuelings, would leave the four men weary and stiff.

Andrew Air Force Base, Maryland

A raw wind accosted the Prowler as it touched down on Runway 19L of Andrews Air Force Base, the tires screeching when rubber met concrete surface. The jet shuddered as Connelly threw the two powerful Pratt & Whitney engines into reverse, the force of the landing jolting all four men forward against their seat harnesses. Smoke and debris, caught by the wind, propelled outward from the tires, further blackening the remnants of a recent snowstorm laying in scattered piles along the edges of the runway.

Oblivious to the deafening noise pervading the aircraft, Grant stared out the port side canopy of the rear seat. But it was an empty stare, with questions and decisions racing through his mind. Where was he supposed to start? He'd have to get the okay from somebody.

He and Adler stepped down onto the tarmac and into a cold, fifteen knot wind smacking against their faces, the wind chill factor was seven degrees above zero. They stood by the jet as the navigator handed them their flight bags. "Thanks for the lift," Grant said, shaking hands with Connelly then with Lieutenant(j.g.) Gomez.

"Our pleasure, sir," responded Lieutenant Connelly, "just sorry the in-flight service wasn't up to par." He elbowed the navigator in the ribs and laughed.

Grant forced a smile without responding. He had too much on his mind. Adler shot him a sideways glance, then answered Connelly. "Uh, no problem, sir. We enjoyed the flight. Thanks for getting us safely back on home soil."

Grant started to leave, then said as an afterthought, "Listen, we'll get these flight suits and jackets back to you." Without waiting for a reply, he started walking away.

"No rush, sir," Connelly answered, his voice trailing as he looked questioningly at Adler.

"Come on, Chief," Grant called over his shoulder.

Both men pulled the fur collars up around their ears, Adler holding his arm close against his body, preventing unnecessary motion inside the sling. Their pace quickened and they made a dash across the runway. On the concrete sidewalk, patches of ice glistened under the harsh lighting of the entrance to the Operations building.

Grant held the door open for the Chief. "Come on, Joe, we've got shit to do."

They went down the deserted main hallway, their footsteps echoing on the polished, hard flooring. Finding the men's room around the corner of the first passageway, they changed into their uniforms then continued down the hall. A black arrow on the sign at the bottom of the stairway pointed up to the main Operation's office on the second floor.

Grant could only hope that Buckley was in. He knew there was a secure phone in the office and Buckley was the perfect choice. He and Commander Stuart Buckley first met in Vietnam when Buckley was a Sea Wolf helo pilot. The last time they saw one another was in Coronado. Stu was a helo pilot attached to North Island supporting the students and Grant was teaching 'tadpoles' at school.

"Jesus," Adler said as he shivered, "I'm still cold. How 'bout a cup of coffee before we go in, sir?"

"No," Grant answered sharply. He immediately regretted his response and shook his head.

"Sorry, Joe, I didn't mean that the way it sounded. You know we've gotta get this done."

"I know, sir."

They walked to the large double doors marked "Operation's Office." Both men removed their caps, tucking them under their arms.

As Grant reached for the handle, Adler stopped him. "Commander, this is gonna mean..."

Grant nodded. "Yeah, Chief."

The large Operation's Office consisted of rows of metal desks, some back to back with tall gray file cabinets lining two walls. The bright overhead lighting was in sharp contrast to the dull decor. Although only a few earlybirds were in the office, the sound of ringing telephones continued to intermingle with clicking typewriters keys and slamming file drawers. Nothing appeared to distract or change the flow of business.

Grant and Adler maneuvered around three rows of desks, then turned toward the glass-enclosed office. A stocky man, shorter than Grant, with gray, short cropped hair, was in the outer office with his back to them, talking to his secretary. "Peggy, pull those two down off the board and send them to the south hangar. They're due for A&P inspection."

"I'll take care of it, Stu," replied Peggy Harrelson as she made a notation on the steno pad.

"Hey, Stu!" Grant called as he pushed the door open further.

Buckley's blue eyes widened when he turned and saw Grant, immediately flashing a broad grin.

"Well, you ol' snake-eater! Where've you been?" Their hands slapped together in a firm, friendly handshake. He nodded, acknowledging Adler.

"This is Senior Chief Joe Adler, Stu," Grant said.

Adler and Buckley shook hands, Buckley asking, "Didn't you use to be with the Teams, Chief?"

"Yes, sir," Adler smiled.

Buckley turned back to Grant. "This is quite an occasion. You've gotta want something bad," he laughed. "When a steely-eyed, trained jungle fighter isn't in his camies, he's lookin' for a favor!"

"You're right, Stu. We've gotta talk."

Buckley's smile gradually faded, noticing a disturbed expression on Grant's face, detecting a somber tone in his voice. "Peggy, we can pick this up later this morning."

"Alright, Stu. I'll go check on the report Frank's putting together." The veteran secretary picked up her stenography notebook from the edge of the desk. She nodded to the two strangers as she passed by them, closing the office door behind her.

Stu turned his attention back to Grant, placing a hand against his friend's back. "Let's go into my office."

A brief conversation took place, Grant relaying a minimal amount of information. "I'd like to use the scramble phone, Stu."

"Sure. No problem. You want I should leave?"

"It'd be best."

"Understood. I'll go get a cup of coffee." Stu

noticed Adler giving an almost pleading look in Grant's direction, so he asked, "How do ya take your java, Chief?"

"Black, sir. Thanks."

Stu started opening the door. "How 'bout you, Grant?"

Grant sat with his elbows resting on his knees, his chin leaning against his fists. He shook his head, not even looking up.

For several moments, Grant and Adler sat quietly in the office, Grant finally dialing the secure number he knew by heart, the number of the Secretary of Defense.

Office of the SECDEF

Allington's staff had not yet arrived, except for his secretary, Francine. He answered the intercom. "Yes, Francine."

"There's a Commander Stevens on line one."

"Thanks, Francine." He pressed the blinking yellow button. "Commander Stevens! Where are you?" he responded with surprise.

"I'm calling from the Op Center at Andrews, sir."

Allington shuffled through the scattered papers on his cluttered desk. "Morelli and I spoke, but I don't recall him saying when you were coming back, Commander, or did I just miss something?"

"No, sir, I didn't give a specific time. And you're the only one in the chain of command that I've spoken with since I've been back." Grant cleared his throat. "A situation has developed that I feel requires your personal attention, sir," he said running a hand over the top of his head. "I need to speak to you and the National Security Advisor. It's a matter of deep concern and one of national security, sir."

Allington coughed and sat forward, resting his arms on his desk, while eyeing the empty pot of coffee on the credenza. "Do you want me to put you on scramble?"

"No, sir. I'd rather not discuss this any further over any phone. We need to meet face-to-face, as soon as possible, sir."

Allington took a deep breath. He knew Grant wasn't given to dramatics. This had to be something heavy. "Hmm. I see." The SecDef ran his pencil along the page of the leather covered appointment book, nearly every line filled for that day. He adjusted his glasses, looking through the bifocals. "There's a 9 o'clock meeting at the Japanese embassy. Those things never start on time, anyway, if you needed extra time. How does 'as soon as you can get here' sound?"

Grant glanced up at the overhead wall clock showing 0715 hours. "That'll be fine, sir, but it shouldn't take long. I just need your guidance, and that of the President's."

"Hold on a minute, Commander." He pressed the intercom button. "Francine, try and find Allan Wooster. Let me know immediately when you do." On the line again with Grant, he said, "My secretary will try and locate Alan Wooster, but we may have no choice other than to put him on the scrambler. Will that do, Commander?"

"Yes, sir." Grant looked over at Adler, who was massaging his sore shoulder. "Senior Chief Adler is with me, sir. He'll be able to corroborate what I'm going to discuss with you. He played a major part in a successful mission, sir."

"Yes, that's what I understand. I'd like an overview today on that situation, Commander, before the official inquiry. Will that be possible?"

"Yes, sir."

Francine cracked open the office door and Allington looked up. "Hang on, Commander." He covered the phone as his secretary relayed a message. "Commander? Wooster's on the other line. Hold on." After a brief moment, Allington got back to Grant. "Commander, Wooster will be here."

"Thank you, sir. The Senior Chief and I will leave immediately."

Allington swiveled his chair around, staring out his office window from the fourth floor of the Pentagon. On the southwest side, beyond the George Washington Parkway, the street and house lights of Crystal City began to lose their glitter in the cold morning's early light.

He loosened his blue paisley tie, then unbuttoned the top button of his white Oxford shirt. "Alright, Commander. You're very serious, aren't you?"

"Yes, sir, I am. As I said, it's a matter of national security."

After hanging up the phone, Allington stood by the window, then turned when he heard the door open.

Francine stood in the doorway, curling one side of her chin length, auburn hair behind her ear. "Would you like me to put on a pot of coffee?"

"You can read my mind, Francine. Oh, by the way, I know you were planning on doing some research in the library this morning, but would you mind staying in the office for awhile?"

"Not at all," she responded as she walked to the credenza and picked up the percolator. "I'll just give Pete a call. This will be a good excuse for him to take me to an early lunch." She smiled and left.

Within a short while Francine announced that Grant and Adler had arrived. "Send them in," Allington said. He glanced over at the National Security Advisor.

Wooster sat in the leather chair with one leg crossed over the other. He nervously tapped his fingers on the armrest.

Thirty minutes later, Grant was wrapping up a full explanation on the events leading up to Donovan's death and the sinking of the trawler. The SecDef and National Security Advisor drilled both Grant and Adler, not leaving a stone unturned.

When all questions were asked and answered, Wooster finally said, "Commander Stevens, the Secretary said you mentioned you had a security issue to discuss."

Everyone focused on Grant as he began, "Mr.

Secretary, Mr. Wooster, this is going to be very difficult for me." He got up and slipped one hand into a pocket of his dress blues trousers. "Very difficult," he said quietly under his breath. Out of the corner of his eye he saw Adler straighten in the chair.

Grant started talking, his voice deep and controlled. "I'd like you to cast aside the areas of coincidence and look at everything through a non-jaundiced eye." The men nodded. "As you know, Admiral Morelli and I were stationed briefly at the American Embassy in Moscow during the NATO Strategy meetings back in '70. The Admiral had requested that I take the security chief position when I expressed an interest in staying in intelligence.

"There were official receptions following the meetings. Sergei Vernichenko was in attendance at the meetings and receptions." Grant glanced momentarily out the window, then lowered his head, before looking again at Allington. "Sir, I personally observed Vernichenko and Admiral Morelli leave the receptions together and not return until approximately one hour later."

"Commander," Wooster growled quietly as he stared at Grant through squinted eyes.

"Please, sir, please. I just ask that you hear me out." Wooster sat back again.

Allington's voice was just louder than a whisper. "I assume you spoke to the Admiral immediately about your concern, Commander."

"Actually, sir, the Admiral approached me with

an explanation."

Wooster uncrossed his legs and leaned forward. "And what was that, Commander?"

"Vernichenko had been with the KGB only a short time, sir. The CIA said they received intel from the inside, making them believe that Vernichenko was willing to become a double agent. The Admiral said he had instructions to make contact with him."

Wooster stood by his chair, sliding his foot back and forth along an invisible line on the deep, blue carpet. "And didn't that sit right with you, Commander?" his tone slapping with cynicism.

Grant brought himself to his full height, at least seven inches above Wooster's. "At the time, sir, it was a very reasonable explanation. As I said, I was new to the position, still learning, and the Admiral was my boss. But I did file away the incident," he said pointing to his head. "It's a habit I learned early on, sir."

He took a few steps toward Adler, then turned. "Plans for the *Bronson* were well past the drawing board stage when the first meeting was held in Moscow, sirs. You're already aware that the Admiral was part of the initial design team for the ship."

"He was one of many, Commander," commented a clearly agitated Allan Wooster.

"Of course, sir, but it's also fact that Admiral Morelli and Vernichenko have crossed paths numerous times since 1970. We also know that very few...very few men had the codes for the *Bronson*." He smacked his fist into his palm with each statement. "The commandos knew the codes. They knew their way around that ship like they had a diagram."

Allington swung his chair around toward the window, then back, as he asked, "Commander, is there any evidence Admiral Morelli knew Donovan personally, I mean, beyond Navy business?"

Grant shook his head slowly and responded, "No, sir. I haven't been able to find any evidence of that. It's my belief that he was never aware of Donovan being the mole. That's just the way the Russians operate, sir--on a need to know basis." He paused, running a hand across his forehead. "After Senior Chief Adler and I had the confrontation with the Russian commandos aboard the *Bronson*, I was positive it went beyond Donovan, and...I...started pulling out incidents, faces, trying to make a connection.

"I gave certain information to Commander Simmons to pass along to the Admiral, leaving out significant details. Then, when I parachuted onto the trawler, I can tell you that the Russians were waiting--they knew someone was coming. I tried to dig out more info from Vernichenko. His response to my saying we took care of the mole was that 'even though one cuts off the head of a snake, you still don't know how far the body stretches.'" Grant hesitated, allowing the two men to absorb his words.

Allington pressed his palms together, resting his chin on his fingertips. "Why would he take such a risk, Commander? Why would a man with his background, his rank, throw it all away to betray his country?"

Grant sat on the edge of the chair. He rubbed his temple, feeling the roughness of the stitches against his fingertips, and he shook his head, responding, "I can't answer that, sir."

"You can't answer that, Commander?" Wooster asked in a sarcastic, thunderous voice. "You're accusing the Chief of Naval Investigative Service, a United States Navy Admiral, of treason, and you can't answer?"

"Sir, right now I can only tell you that putting the facts together, it makes sense to me."

Adler blinked, catching the comment, thinking to himself, Ouch! Be careful, sir. He tried to be inconspicuous as he wiped perspiration from his upper lip.

Grant stood again. "Sirs, the only way I can prove it is to confront the Admiral."

Wooster tapped his finger against his mouth. "And don't you also mean possibly 'disprove', Commander?"

Grant nodded. "Sir, if I'm wrong, my resignation will be on your desk by tomorrow. I'll make a public apology to the Admiral." He lowered his head, saying quietly, "But I don't think I'm wrong, sir." He jerked his head up, staring at Allington. "Sir, this isn't easy for me. I'm the last one you'll ever meet who wants any of this to be true. I've agonized over this, sir."

Allington focused his eyes on Adler, sitting quietly, staring at Grant. Adler was the only one who understood what Grant was going through, and he nodded.

Grant walked closer to the SecDef. "If I face him, sir, I'll know...we'll all know one way or other."

Wooster slapped the arm of the upholstered wing chair. "Goddamnit, Commander! You know and I know that a public apology or your resignation won't be near enough if you're wrong. The whole Navy will take a hit. How would you repair Morelli's career after the word leaks...and it will leak, you know."

"What you're really asking, sir, is if I'm wrong, how would I explain this to the President."

Wooster sat back, resting his forefinger against his long, thin nose, rubbing an imaginary itch. "Something like that." He rose from the chair slowly. "Look, you'd better be right, Stevens, 'cause a wrong answer from Morelli, and we'll nail your salty ass to a yardarm. Am I making myself perfectly clear?"

Grant brought himself to attention. "Yes, sir...crystal clear, sir." Grant was somewhat insulted by the National Security Advisor's skepticism, but knew he was a long-time fan of Morelli's and was instrumental in securing his appointment at NIS.

Allington was clearly unprepared for the conversation and accusations that had just been thrown around the room. But for whatever reason, there was something about Grant Stevens, making him positive that a resignation wouldn't be a forthcoming event. "Uh, Commander, you do what you have to do. Call me the minute your meeting is over."

"Yes, sir."

The SecDef walked around from behind his desk. "Commander, if you have to call the Admiral's office to tell him you're on your way, you can use the phone in the outer office."

"No need, sir. I directed Commander Simmons to send word to him after Senior Chief Adler and I left the carrier, advising the Admiral we'd be back sometime today."

Adler sat quietly throughout most of the proceeding. As he stood, Allington walked over to him. "Senior Chief, Commander Stevens had some very good words about you. We thank you for everything you did."

Adler stood tall. "Thank you, sir." He nodded toward Grant. "And Commander Stevens."

Naval Investigative Service - 1005 hours

"Commander Stevens!" Petty Officer Gardner slammed the file cabinet drawer next to him. "Welcome back, sir."

"Thanks, Alex." Grant removed his coat and laid it over the back of the chair. He motioned in Adler's direction. "This is Senior Chief Adler." Hardly pausing, he asked, "Is the Admiral in?"

"Yes, sir. Let me tell him you're here." Gardner disappeared behind the office door.

Grant put his cap on the edge of the desk, then looked up at Adler. "Joe,--"

"I'll wait for you out here, sir."

Gardner held the door open. "Commander, the Admiral will see you."

Grant gave a quick sideways look at Adler before he walked into the office. Once behind the closed door, Grant stared hard at his long-time friend, taking a few steps closer to the desk. He saluted. "Sir."

Morelli stood and returned Grant's salute, then he came from behind his desk. He reached out to shake Grant's hand. "You did a remarkable job, Commander."

"Thank you, sir."

"How are you feeling?" he asked as he pointed to the stitches.

Grant stood at ease, bringing his arms behind his back. "I...I'm fine, sir."

Morelli looked toward his office door, then back at Grant. "Is Senior Chief Adler with you?"

"Yes, sir, he is."

"Hmm. Commander Simmons informed me the chief was injured."

"Yes, sir, he was. He took a bullet in the shoulder. But he'll be okay, sir."

"Good. Good." Morelli turned away, then picked up his cigar before sitting behind the desk. "Well, Grant, I know you have something on your mind. Talk to me."

Grant stepped closer to the desk that he and Morelli had so many conversations across. He looked directly into Gene Morelli's bloodshot eyes. "I'm right, aren't I, sir?" What seemed like a few very long, agonizing seconds passed as the two men stared at each other. "Christ! I'm right," Grant said with affirmation, his voice trailing off. Morelli inhaled a lungful of smoke-filled air, a vacant stare in his eyes.

Grant stood rigid, his arms stiff by his sides. His head was throbbing. He couldn't remember a time he'd felt so confused, so disillusioned. He massaged his temple as he walked to the window with Morelli watching him. Turning suddenly, he blurted out, "It started when you approached Vernichenko during the Moscow conference, didn't it?"

Morelli shook his head ever so slightly. "I had a contact right here at the Russian Embassy. That was the beginning." He tilted his head and ran a finger up and down behind his ear. When he spoke it was more like a man astonished, not like one being a braggart or pretentious. "It was so easy, Grant. All our security measures, intel, background checks...they all meant squat. It was so very easy."

Grant could guess how Morelli managed to defy the intelligence networks, how he passed the information, but he wanted to know more. "Why? Why, sir? How the hell could you do it?" For a brief moment he noticed a softening around Morelli's eyes, his face relaxing. Immediately, Grant knew and he stepped back, staring at Morelli through squinted eyes. "Your son? Because of what happened to Jimmy?"

The Admiral's calm facial expression instantly

flashed cold, icy hostility, changing as quickly as flipping over a playing card, as drastically as night turning to day. He smacked the desk with his large, heavy hand, catching Grant by surprise, who blinked and snapped his head back as Morelli's voice rose to a dull roar. "They owed me, Grant! They owed me. Thirty goddamn years of my life I gave them, never asking or questioning. Was it so difficult, so impossible for them to do one favor for me, or for Jimmy?"

"But, Jesus Christ, sir--"

Morelli didn't give him an opportunity to finish, as his voice thundered, "They didn't have to give him those orders to Ben Cat. I requested that he be assigned to a more secure base." He slumped against his chair, suddenly sounding like a man broken, a man who had managed to hide his anguish and rage for so long, from so many. "You knew Jimmy. You saw my grief. He was my only son...my only child." He paused, taking several long breaths. "And you know my wife died three months after him."

Silence, deep and brooding, hung over the office like a thick, black shroud. Grant nodded his head slowly, feeling the ache deep inside him, an unrelenting pain that left an empty space ever since Jenny died. There were times he could almost smell the fragrance of her perfume, imagine the silkiness of her long, brown hair flowing through his fingers. He jerked his head up, the Admiral's voice severing his thoughts, bringing reality back.

"The doctors said Miriam lost her will to live. She died of a broken heart, Grant." He rubbed his hand back and forth under his jaw. "The two most important people in my life...gone."

"I know, sir, and I'm...sorry." Grant backed away from the desk, almost in shock. His long-time friend was no longer the person he knew. But why couldn't he have noticed something was wrong? Why didn't he see it? All the years they had known one another, Morelli had somehow been able to hide his depression and bitterness like a genuine master of deception.

Grant Stevens was feeling acute pangs of guilt over his inability to have helped his long-time friend and mentor. But his guilt ran deep, deep enough to change his emotion to anger, as he began taking on the blame for the whole *Bronson* incident. If he had helped Morelli, it never would have happened and Seaman Koosman would still be alive. As with Donovan, Grant could only see the uniform of a Navy admiral, the man inside it, a traitor.

Now, he wanted to strike back. "Jesus Christ! Jimmy wanted to go, and he wasn't the only one who died over there. In case you've forgotten, Admiral, you sent a helluva lot of men to Nam who never came back. What gives you the goddamn right to blame anybody?" He watched Morelli, studying a face twisted with grief, now shocked by Grant's reaction. "And why did you send me on this assignment, Admiral? You had to know I'd find out."

Regaining his composure, Morelli reached for the burning cigar in the ashtray, holding the panatela by its familiar orange, white and black band. "You still don't see." A thick cloud of cigar smoke swirled toward the ceiling. "I know you. I knew you wouldn't let them get away with it. I had to see it through, and I knew you wouldn't stop until you put all the pieces of the puzzle together.

"Like I said before, Grant...you're the best. I counted on it being you. I wanted it to be you, don't you realize that? I built these last few years at the expense of many of my fellow officers, Grant, just to be here at this moment in time. You were the key to ending this. Remember when I asked you to be prepared to destroy the trawler, to make it look like an accident?"

"Yes, sir." Grant took a step away from the desk, kneading the muscles in the back of his neck.

"Your instinct told you what you had to do, didn't it?"

"I suppose it did."

"And you got to settle an old score, besides." Grant nodded. "Exactly. And that's what I counted on."

"And what if I didn't, Admiral, what if I didn't?"

Morelli's lips curled into somewhat of a smile. "Then, Commander, we would have blown all the fuckers out of the water." Not taking his eyes from Grant, he added, "The trawler and the sub, Commander."

Another affirmation, Grant thought. That was

one of the details he didn't relay, information about a Russian sub being involved in the plot.

"It still doesn't make sense," he said, shaking his head. Then he turned sharply, unable to control his anger, continuously pounding his fist on the desk. "You were willing to give them the *Bronson*! Give them the technology of the most advanced, destructive weapon in the world! You risked everything, endangered lives...betrayed your country." He leaned toward Morelli, coming face-to-face with him, smelling the odor of tobacco on his breath. "And now you're trying to say you weren't going to let them get away with it from the beginning?"

Morelli flicked white ashes toward the ashtray, some scattering across the green blotter. He took slow, deliberate steps toward the window, momentarily staring across the parking lot, before turning back to face Grant as he leaned against the windowsill. "I didn't say that. I've carried my anger for many years, an anger strong enough to have let it happen. You see, I had it all planned, and I didn't give a flying fuck what happened to me--court martial, prison, hanging--nothing mattered. I would have my revenge." He held the cigar out in front of him, and shook it slowly at Grant. "That is, I had it all planned, right up until your confrontation with Donovan."

Grant cocked his head to the side, his brow wrinkling. "What did that have to do with it?"

Morelli's body suddenly seemed to weigh a thousand pounds, taking additional effort for him to walk toward the younger officer, whose face still showed genuine bewilderment, disbelief, but most of all, anger.

Morelli's voice wavered. He put his hand on Grant's shoulder. "When I found out what happened, I saw Jimmy's face again. You could've been killed. And I placed you in that situation."

Right before Grant's eyes, Gene Morelli seemed to have aged twenty years in the span of a few seconds.

Grant shook his head as he backed away. "I took the risk, sir, from day one. That's part of my job. It wasn't the first time, Admiral, that you've sent me on mission critical jobs. And it sure as hell won't be the last."

"I'm aware of that, but this time it was because of me, because of my personal vendetta. It hit me like a speeding freight train, and...I'm sorry."

Grant snapped back. "Sorry? If you're sorry, why the hell did you tell the Russians about my plan to parachute onto the trawler?" Grant's anger was unmistakable. He kept his eyes glued to Morelli's face.

Morelli turned his head and stared out the window as if trying to avoid an answer. "We've known each other too long, Grant, for me not to know how you think. You do things by the book--most of the time--and as they say, you never leave a stone unturned. I knew you were after more information, to confirm what you already suspected."

He looked down, watching the cigar as he rolled it between his fingers. Then, he raised his eyes, staring at Grant. "The Russians didn't know who--only when. And they didn't know about Donovan being dead, did they?"

Grant tilted his head back and closed his eyes, then he looked at Morelli again. "You were 'broad-casting' your final flash message...so I would find out."

Morelli walked around him and went to the window. He took a deep breath. His voice was barely audible when he asked, "Can you forgive me, Grant?"

Grant's back stiffened. "Hell, no! No way, sir!"

Morelli's shoulders slumped; he turned sharply and went behind his desk. He crushed the cigar in the ashtray, stared at it for a moment, then let it drop. Grant followed his every move.

The Admiral finally sat in his leather chair. He grabbed the edge of the desk and rolled himself closer. He looked up, and when he spoke, it was in his official tone of voice. "You know you have a job to do, Commander."

Grant lifted his cap off the desk, then walked toward the door. Morelli couldn't see the muscles in his jaw twitching. He was oblivious to the turmoil tearing apart Grant's insides. Holding his cap by the brim, Grant stared down at the eagle emblem, lightly running his fingers over it before he said over his shoulder. "Wrong, Admiral. This is one job you're gonna have to finish yourself."

Morelli sat somberly, his arms hanging limp at his sides. It looked as if he was staring into a black hole, his world being sucked deeper into it, and he was trying desperately to see a light beyond it.

Grant turned and left the office, closing the door securely behind him. He leaned back heavily, his hands balled up into tight fists.

Adler stood, very concerned seeing Grant so visibly shaken. "Skipper? What can I--"

The loud, sharp, classic explosion of a model 1917 military .45 smashed the silence in the outer office. Yeoman Gardner spun around from the file cabinet, making a dash to the office door.

Grant stood his ground, stopping the panic-stricken young petty officer in his tracks. Grant's voice sounded hoarse as he said, "Yeoman, call the Shore Patrol's office, then the SecDef and National Security Advisor."

Gardner tugged on the knot of his Navy scarf, panic covering his ashen face. His blue eyes darted back and forth from Grant to the Chief. He grabbed the brass doorknob. "But, sir--"

"That's an order, Petty Officer!"

Startled, the young sailor released his death grip on the doorknob, then took a step back, still staring at Grant who motioned toward the desk. "Yes, sir," he finally responded, then reluctantly, went to his desk with its stacks of organized folders and glass container of sharpened pencils. His hand shook as he picked up the phone and dialed the number of the Shore Patrol Officer.

Adler stood stone-still in the middle of the room. "Christ, Commander!"

Grant put on his cap, adjusted it squarely, then drew his shoulders back. "Don't let anyone in till the Shore Patrol gets here, Chief."

"Sir?"

"I'm gonna get some air, Joe, and wait for Wooster."

Adler stepped aside as Grant walked past and he responded, "Yes, sir."

Chapter Eleven

Thursday, February 5

With his black, nylon gym bag slung over his shoulder, Grant slammed the car door, then unzipped his windbreaker. He looked overhead through dark, aviator sunglasses at a cobalt-colored sky. The warmth from the early morning sun felt good on his face. February was starting out better than its usual, blustery self. The dark circles under his eyes had faded and the black stitches had been removed from his head. All that remained was a thin, raised scar. It was amazing what a few days leave could do for mind and body.

The phone rang just as he walked into his room at the BOQ. "Stevens."

"Commander Stevens?"

"Yes, ma'am."

"Commander, this is Emily at Secretary Canon's office. The Secretary would like you to come to his office at 10 AM. Can you make it?"

He dropped his gym bag on the floor, glancing at his watch. "Yes, ma'am. I'll be there."

Weaving the black Vette in and out of traffic Grant could merely speculate on why he'd been called to the Secretary of the Navy's office. Monday had been a full day spent at the inquiry and then debriefing. None of the reasons popping into his mind seemed logical.

Twenty minutes later, and wearing a new set of Navy dress blues, he was standing at attention before Secretary John Canon.

"At ease, Commander, and just drop your cap on the chair." Grant complied, then the Secretary walked around from behind the walnut desk and stood in front of him. "Commander, I'd like to present this Legion of Merit Medal to you." The medal hung from a wide, magenta-colored ribbon with a narrow white stripe down each edge.

"Thank you, sir," Grant replied, as he shook Canon's hand.

Canon stepped back as he remarked, "But Commander, I have to tell you, I believe you're out of uniform."

Grant instantaneously went through a mental check list of his uniform and was hesitant to look down. "Excuse me, sir?"

The Secretary leaned over the desk and pulled out the bottom left hand drawer, removing two shoulder boards, each with four gold stripes. He held them out in front of Grant. "I believe these are yours, Captain."

Grant's shoulders went slack. "Sir, I, I--Captain?"

Canon reached for Grant's hand, then put the shoulder boards across his palm. "I have a note here that I'd like to read to you." He picked up the white bond paper and unfolded it, the presidential seal emblazoned across the top. 'To: Commander Grant Stevens, United States Navy. It gives me great pleasure to inform you that you have been approved for selection to the rank of Captain in the United States Navy, effective immediately, pending your successful physical examination and acceptance of this rank, and in accordance with Naval Regulation', etc., etc. I'm sure you know the rest. And, of course, it's signed, President Samuel McNeely."

By now, Grant was again standing at attention, the words ringing in his ears. "Thank you, sir! And the President, too, sir. I...I really don't know what else to say."

Canon nodded. "Captain Stevens, I don't want this to sound trite, but we are the ones who thank you for your service to your country. You took great risks and followed through to the end, knowing full well the consequences."

Grant bit his bottom lip. It would be a long time before the sound would quit hammering against his brain. Because of his anger, he and he alone was responsible for Gene Morelli taking his own life. He told himself repeatedly that he did what was right, but it was difficult to unravel his feelings. The initial guilt he felt for being unable to help Morelli had quickly changed to anger. That anger would stay bottled up in him a long time, but it was the years of friendship that kept getting in the way of his understanding. His long-time friend had betrayed him.

"At ease, Captain." Grant complied. Canon folded his arms across his chest and leaned against the desk. "I believe I know what you're feeling and thinking at this moment." He studied Grant's face for a moment. "You know, it was pure chance I came across a quote by Ulysses S. Grant yesterday, and I'd like to relay it to you now. 'Let no guilty man escape, if it can be avoided. No personal considerations should stand in the way of performing a duty.'"

Grant stared straight ahead. "Thank you, sir."

Just then, the intercom buzzer sounded and Canon pressed the button. "Yes?"

"Your next appointment is here, Mr. Secretary," announced Emily Shorter from the outer office.

"Ah, yes, send him in, Emily."

Joe Adler walked in, a surprised look on his and Grant's face. He saluted, then asked with a broad grin, "Sir, what are you doing here?"

Grant held out his hand with the new shoulder boards. "The Secretary said I was out of uniform until I put these on, Joe! You believe it?"

Adler rushed to his friend, his hand outstretched. "Congratulations, sir! Outstanding! I knew this was gonna be a good day!" Even though his arm was finally free of the sling, he still had some mild pain in his shoulder, but he ignored it and continued vigorously shaking Grant's hand.

Grant laughed. "I suppose you got that twitch in your neck again?"

"Like I told you before, sir--it works!"

Canon smiled, listening to the easy conversation passing between the two friends. He reached into his side jacket pocket, looking at the medal with an eagle, hanging from a green ribbon with two white stripes. "Joe, front and center," he called, as he waved Adler toward him.

"Sir," Adler said, standing at attention.

"Joe, I'd like to present you with this Navy Commendation Medal." He pinned the medal to Adler's dress blues jacket. "Thank you, Senior Chief."

"Thank you, sir."

Canon lifted a blue box from his desk. "Stay where you are, Joe." He handed the box to Grant. "Captain, I think you should have the honor."

Grant opened the lid. He snapped his head up first to look at Canon, then at Adler, a broad grin immediately flashing across his face. "Joe! Your neck twitching again?"

Adler's brow furrowed. "Sir?" Grant held the open box in front of him. Adler's blue eyes went to the size of dinner plates when he saw the silver bars. "Shit, sir! I...! What...! Not me, sir!"

Canon practically fell against his desk from laughing so hard. There had been very few times during the past months that the Secretary of the Navy heard laughter in his office.

Grant pinned the bars on Adler's collar then grabbed his hand. "Congratulations, Lieutenant(j.g.) Adler! And now, I believe you're out of uniform, Mister!"

Handshakes went all around before the Secretary of the Navy finally said, "Gentlemen, have a seat so we can discuss some business," and he motioned toward the couch. "Can I get you something to drink?" Grant and Adler both declined. "Captain, your new assignment will be as Chief of Staff at NIS. Lieutenant Adler is being assigned as your aide."

"Sir, excuse me, but before we go any further, may I make a recommendation concerning the *Bronson*?"

"Of course, Captain." Canon sat back, crossed his legs, and smoothed his blue pin-striped trousers.

"Well, sir, we've got the 'only game in town' with that ship, and with the Cold War situation as it is, someone is bound to try again."

"Captain, don't you think the odds are pretty slim of there being another mole?"

"Yes, sir, but there are many ways for it to happen."

"What do you suggest?"

"Sir, I believe you should assign a squad of SEALs from Team 1. Agent Mullins has made that same recommendation, sir."

Canon raised an eyebrow, but there appeared to be somewhat of a smile on his lips. "What, no Marines, Captain? You aren't just being biased here, are you?"

"Maybe somewhat, sir, but I strongly believe they'd be your best defense for the ship."

"I'm sure the Appropriations Committee will ask, but wouldn't that mean a major overhaul to accommodate them?"

Grant shook his head. "It shouldn't be, sir. The after repair bay could be converted into a galley and bunkroom."

"Isn't there already a galley on board?"

"The galley Agent Mullins uses is on 03 level, sir, the same level as the communication's center. I think you'd want the team to be closer to topside security."

"Sir, may I say something?" Adler asked. Canon nodded. "Sir, I agree with the Comman...I mean, the Captain. It seemed awfully easy for those Russians to board. If we hadn't been there, sir, Agent Mullins wouldn't have had a chance and the *Bronson* would most likely be destroyed."

"Appreciate your input, Joe. Is there anything else?" he asked as looked back and forth between the two men.

"Yes, sir," Grant replied, "but one more thing. I suggest that you let it be known that the SEALs are on board."

Canon stood and slipped his hand into his pocket. "Would that be wise, Captain?"

"I believe so, sir. If the other side knows, their only option would be a direct strike and that would be an act of outright aggression, which could mean war. This incident was as close as it came, sir. We were lucky this time."

"Point well taken," Canon nodded. "I guess your first assignment at NIS will be to start putting the wheels in motion for this to happen, and I'll do what I have to do. Right now, you both need to go over there and start picking up the pieces before your new boss arrives."

Grant nodded in acknowledgment and asked, "Do you know who it will be, sir?"

"We have a few names in mind, but actually, we hoped you would make a recommendation."

"Well, sir, there are some good men out there from the Teams. If you want someone with covert background--"

"That's exactly who we're looking for," Canon interrupted as he walked behind his desk. "It seems that recent world situations are leading more and more to those types of encounters."

"I'd recommend Admiral Torrinson, sir. He's at WARCOM."

"Hmm. Very well, Captain. I'll pass that along to the President." Canon made a note on his desk pad, then walked back toward the two men, who stood immediately. "Gentlemen, congratulations again. And, Joe, you need to keep your boss out of trouble, you hear?"

Adler grinned. "Yes, sir. I've done it before!"

They left the office and Grant motioned, "Come on, Joe, I'll give you a ride to NIS. We may as well get started."

He unlocked the Vette's passenger side door then walked around the back. Adler rested his hand on the car's shiny, black roof, glistening in the sunlight.

Grant was slipping on his sunglasses when Adler asked, "Think my Mustang can give you a run for your money, sir?"

"Take you on any time, friend! As soon as you

get that 'horse' here, I'll take you to a perfect place for us to spin our wheels!"

Grant opened the door and tossed his cap in the back. They both settled into the black leather bucket seats. He turned the ignition key and the Vette's powerful engine roared, responding immediately.

Adler cocked his head to the side and grinned, loving the sound of a racing engine. "You know what this means, don't you, sir, I mean about the two of us being assigned to NIS?"

Grant shook his head. "No, but I expect you're gonna tell me."

"Well, sir, it seems evident that they're just making it all the more easier for us to get into trouble together!"

Grant threw the gearshift into first, popped the clutch, and the wide, rubber tires smoked and squealed as he pulled away from the curb, leaving black streaks down a length of pavement.

"Yeah, Joe. Life's good!"

Made in the USA
Lexington, KY
01 October 2014